Don't Chuck Me Out

Also by Millicent Jones
Footsteps
Camden Haven Cameo
Yearning
The Bird of Time

Millicent Jones

Don't Chuck Me Out

To my children
To save you hours of chucking out!

Don't Chuck Me Out
ISBN 978 1 76041 726 0
Copyright © Millicent Jones 2019

First published 2019 by
GINNINDERRA PRESS
PO Box 3461 Port Adelaide 5015
www.ginninderrapress.com.au

Contents

An After Christmas Story

There were no hassles when the old girl died – well, that is when all the funeral stuff was over. Nobody quibbled about who wanted this or that. It all seemed to fall into place OK. Mind you, she'd labelled various bits and pieces. The Copenhagen china snail for Bertie (we knew he'd always loved it); 'If', the old framed poem by Kipling, left for little Mercy's twenty-first birthday present; the green glass vase, a family relic from the pioneering days, for our eldest bro – fair enough. And so on.

We wandered through the place aware of a quietness, a void, empty now of her presence but filled to overflowing with her life's mementos. Paintings, photos, ornaments – all meaningful to her. Each one could tell a story if it had a voice, and over and over we wondered what those stories were and why we hadn't taken the time to ask or, more to the point, to listen. Too busy with our own important lives to question hers. And no doubt she had probably told us – or tried to – but you know how it is? Preoccupied with the kids and planning futures. Sad excuses. We stared into space, paid lip service to her enthusiastic accounts of this adventure or that mishap. Nodded, pretended to take it in, but soon mumbled, 'Sorry, Ma, have to dash – the kids…' And that would put an end to it. While there was some remorse, there seemed a deeper sense of loss, maybe a loss more of the knowledge of this person who had so shaped our lives, than the actual physical loss itself.

But strangely the one thing that caused some arguments, or should I say heated discussions, was when we pulled out the bags of Christmas decorations from the linen cupboard.

'Oh, look,' says older sis, 'the nativity set. I remember her making that.' She spoke with a distant look in her eyes, rather a reverent look, which struck me as strange considering her present atheist views.

'Come on, sis, you never liked that piece of junk. Heavens, you always complained about the kitsch baby Jesus and the donkey with the broken ear. At least we can give that the heave. Now,' I looked around questioning,' where's the op shop bag?

'Don't be ridiculous,' she flared up. 'She made that. She made it for *us*.'

'You mean she provided a background to go with the carols she played ad infinitum, non-stop for weeks every Christmas. Geez, they drove us all nuts. You most of all.'

'Well, I'm keeping it,' she said. 'Say what you like.'

Then there was the drooping angel that always had pride of place high among the branches because it belonged to her mother's ancient decorations. Once a saintly white and now a dreary cream, minus half a wing and both sets of eyelashes, it really did have to go. I mean, for goodness sake, how soppy can you get?

'But I love that angel,' said little Mercy, and she hugged it to her, stroked the disabled wing as she would an injured bird.

'Forget it, Mercy. We just cannot fly home with extra suitcases of junk. Why, you weren't even born when that crazy daisy first came to light.'

'But I love it,' she repeated.

Oh I hate the reproachful eyes my daughter can act up. I just don't have a chance. Arguments get me nowhere.

'Look at these,' said Adam, as he gently undid the bubble wrap, firmly sticky taped round the gleaming, but somehow jaded, baubles. 'Does anyone remember when she made these?'

Jeff scrambled to his feet. 'Sure do.' He took the largest dazzling purple one. 'God, it's a terrible colour but she thought it was beautiful. And all those pins she kept losing trying to attach these whatnots. And remember how wild she went when the dog started eating them. Oh well...' he shrugged a bit pathetically, 'not really good enough even for the op shop, are they?'

'Hang on a minute, what do you mean, not good enough?' Sally reached out. 'I'll take them.'

'Really, Sal, that's being ridiculous,' said her usually mild mannered mate, but the look she gave him turned his protest into feeble acquiescence. Martin was a firm believer in keeping his wife happy and knew now was certainly not the time to cross swords with her.

Things seemed to be getting a bit tetchy, so I suggested we stop for a break and a cuppa. We'd not long been sipping, lost in our own thoughts (guess this was the first time we had made tea in our mother's house without her being there) when Roger appeared in the courtyard dangling three very bedraggled little red Santas.

'I remember when Granny bought these. I was with her, and we…'

'Shush, darling,' said my big sister, somehow now rather shrunken down to size, 'we're just having a bit of peace and quiet.'

'But Mum, we…'

'*Roger! Please.*'

'Well, I want them,' he whined petulantly, and turned on his heel.

And so it went on – all afternoon. Somebody always had a reason for wanting to keep this piece or that. I found it unfathomable that after we'd managed to agree on, dispense with and dispose of a lifetime of our mother's belongings this strange assortment of bric-a-brac had suddenly become desirable collectables.

And I have to admit that even I, the most hardened of all chucker-outers, was caught in the contest when we came across the silver star. I was determined that the most gaudy of them all would remain in my hands. Brash and flashy, it had vied for top spot with the angel on every Christmas tree, in whatever corner, of whichever house we celebrated in over all those years.

As I held it, I realised it wasn't metal at all but an even tinnier plastic disguised with silver paint. This sparkling symbol of peace and goodwill was at last beginning to chip. I've no idea why this made me tearful but maybe it was the realisation that everything has its time. In the scheme of things, the star had had a good life, as had our mother. She had sparkled gracefully in her prime, even in older years had held sway, but just as the star had begun to lose its lustre, so had she.

I will keep it in my drawer where I hide a few special treasures, one day to be found and pondered on by my own children, and occasionally I will take a peak. Just sometimes when I feel nostalgic. And then all those forgotten memories will tumble out, sparkling like the star. Dear and fragile, I will gather them to me, hold them close and gratefully remember.

Eternity

'What's this old bit of paper?' she asked, perplexed at the wrinkled and stained scrap of envelope she found in my jewel box.

Jewel box we call it but there's not much that would pass for real jewellery. No diamonds or pearls just lots of trinkety stuff I'd collected and worn over the years. The kids, and now the next generation, loved going through it and hearing stories about this and that.

This rainy school holiday day, after many 'pleases' and much pestering, I had finally succumbed and climbed on the chair to hand down the box. We always upended it on the bedroom floor and that's where we were when she asked the question. And followed it with another.

'Why has it got,' she stumbled over the writing, 'E…E…ternity' written on it?

I paused a moment, breathing in the ache I still get in my chest, trying to fight the feeling of being swamped by a strange sense of loneliness whenever I hear the word. Then slowly I began.

'He stood on the corner of Her Majesty's Arcade nearly opposite David Jones and we always saw him there when we went to town. Beside him rested a cardboard sign about two feet high, with the word Eternity written on it in the most perfect, or so I thought, running writing. He always held a tray with many little bits and pieces on it that would catch my eye. I loved to touch and wonder at them all. This day there was the most perfect tiny white china horse with a flowing silver mane and tail. It reminded me of a book I had been reading – *The Silver Brumby – King of the Ranges*. I was captivated by it.

'The shaggy old man had such a nice face and he smiled as he saw my delight.

'"Yes," he said, "it's a very special ornament, it belonged to my mother but," he hesitated, "I need to sell it now."

'Then I saw his sadness and I understood he was poor. Very poor. I had never actually known any really poor people and I wanted desperately to buy the horse, not just for me, but for him too. I eagerly turned to my mother but, as I did, I knocked the tray from the old man's hands.

'Everything scattered onto the pavement. Bounced and tumbled among the shoppers' feet. The china horse shattered into a million pieces. I have never been as mortified as I was that day and in my long life have never felt such shame again. I did all a seven-year-old girl could do – burst into tears. Which, when I saw the look of horror on his face, became a torrent. I remember through the haze my mother bending to help pick up the pieces and fumbling in her purse to pay for the damage. He refusing, she insisting. And then he did a strange thing. He pulled a crumpled envelope from his pocket, took an old piece of pencil from behind his ear, leant over his knee and painstakingly began to write.

'"Here – this is for the little girl, I know she didn't mean to do it."

'When I looked later, there was the word Eternity. I felt lost and puzzled until my mother said *he* was Mr Eternity. She told me afterwards that he had been writing the word with white chalk all over Sydney pavements for years and years. I learnt later he was illiterate and could hardly sign his name, Arthur, but he wrote the word Eternity quite perfectly in beautiful copperplate script. I may have had the only example ever written on paper. It is a strange keepsake I will always cherish and one that leads me to occasionally, quietly, ponder on Isaiah's glorified words.

'It's then I ask myself where did he – and where will we – spend Eternity?'

Excursion

'I'll get her.' Ellen unclipped the seatbelt as the neat little minibus braked outside the retirement village.

'Back the other way – she's in 35,' called Mick the driver.

Several heads belonging to those already collected searched through their windows in a dazed kind of way as Ellen retraced her steps, still unsure, until she spied the unsteady totter of Grace as she grabbed and held fast to her letterbox.

'Ah, there you are. Come on, luv, I'll help you to the bus. Need your stick? Yes, well, I'll carry your bag. There we go now – mind the step.'

Shirley leant out to pull her up and escort her down the aisle to the fifth row. 'What about sitting with Jim today, Grace? My, he's looking handsome in his blue jacket. Quite a catch, and I love your handkerchief, Jim. Very smart.'

'What's that, luv?' says Jim, hand to deaf ear.

'I said you're looking very smart today, Jim. Here's Grace to sit with you. Let's get that seatbelt in place. No, put your arm in here, sweetie – ah, there we go. All set, Mick. Just poor old Ada at the Sweet Dreams village and then we're off.'

It had taken an hour and a quarter to collect all the participants for the monthly outing. Quite an exercise for the volunteers but it was something the oldies looked forward to, so it was time well spent. And of course lunch was always the highlight. Today they were off to the Green Valley Tea House about twenty kilometres out of town and there was much speculation about the food, which, needless to say, was one of the few pleasures left to enjoy for a lot of our old souls.

Picking up Ada took a while since nobody at Sweet Dreams knew where she was. Forgotten the day apparently and wandered off. This had become a problem in recent months, her dementia getting increasingly bad. Ellen finally found her picking roses in her neighbour's garden.

'I'm doin' the flowers,' she said, 'for me daughter's weddin'. She's getting married tomorrer, yer know.'

'Is she now? Well, that's lovely – let's just give them to Maureen here.'

'That damned Ada. She's always picking my flowers,' exploded Maureen.

'Sorry, luv,' soothed Ellen, 'but they'll look lovely in your vase.' And she hustled Ada towards the bus, turning her back on Maureen's expletives.

'Well done, Ell.' Shirley grabbed Ada's hand. 'Let's you and I go down the back and sit in the comfy seats.' Shirley was well aware of the animosity of the others to Ada's incessant rambling, little realising they were not far from that place themselves. But she was tedious and never let up about her daughter's wedding. And she doesn't even have a daughter. Wishful thinking perhaps, as her only son was a dreadful bore and rarely visited.

They were all in their Sunday best – ironed and neat and bejewelled, (except for Ada, of course, who had forgotten the occasion and was wearing her holey cardigan and gardening slippers) and they cheerily continued their gastronomic discussion as they settled down to enjoy the journey.

'They reckon the fish and chips is great.'

'Roast lamb, I heard.'

'Anyone ever been there?'

'We've paid for booze too. Just feel like a beer.'

'Well, I'm for the chocolate mousse. Meant to be something else.'

And so on as they negotiated potholes and curves through delightfully scenic farmland. Recent rain had left the trees glistening and deepened colours.

'Ooh look at those roses – stop, stop. Roses. I need to pick 'em for me daughter's...'

'Aw, come off it, Ada,' yelled an aggravated chorus. 'We're sick of yer bloomin' daughter's wedding.'

'Yes, Ada, let's just look at the countryside and we'll soon be there,' Sheila consoled, 'and I know you like bread and butter custard. I think that's on the menu today.'

All hands were on deck when they arrived – finding sticks and bags and lowering each down the steps with gentle expertise took some time but eventually the little group, several with their walkers, were settled inside and ready to order. All went well until Rupert wanted champagne but he was persuaded that beer was best at midday and raised his bottle to toast. Glasses with wine or port were cheerily tinkled. And Ada? Well, Ada had managed to grab the table decorations, shocking pink plastic roses, and held them triumphantly aloft.

Silence mostly settled around the table while all were busy tucking in. Jim reckoned he'd ordered the sticky date pudding but was happy with the chocolate cheesecake after the first mouthful. 'Geez,' he enthused, 'this is good stuff. Glad they messed me order.'

'Who's for another port,' yodelled Rupert, raising his empty glass.

'I think we'll leave the port,' Sheila intervened. 'Coffee's on the way. And if anyone wants to go to the toilet while we're waiting, it's just out there on the veranda.'

There was an immediate scraping of chairs so a little queuing had to be organised and since the men's was out of order, there was some confusion as to whether the ladies had first go. Jane announced there wasn't any toilet paper left but informed us that at least she'd brought her hankie, which caused some titters among the fellas.

The outing was drawing to an end – Mick was keen to get home to collect his granddaughter from school and gave the horn a discreet toot.

In due course, they were set to go. Frail bodies and walkers and sticks and general good cheer – except for Jane, who grumpily complained someone had taken her place by the window – filled the little bus and with an 'All aboard' from Ellen, they were off.

It was a jovial trip back with scratchy voices lustily singing the old favourites – 'Tipperary', 'Pack Up Your Saddle', 'Daisy', 'I'll Take the High Road' – the only trouble being Ada, who kept calling out that something was missing.

'Don't worry, sweetie – we'll find it when we get back. It'll be somewhere on the bus,' called Ellen over her shoulder. 'We never get old Ada home without her forgetting something, do we?' She leaned over to Shirley.

So despite Ada's constant wailing, they were just about all delivered until it came to Jim.

'Jim! Jim!' called Shirley. 'Come on, Jim, it's your stop. Where are you hiding? Too many goodies, eh? Fallen asleep, I'll bet,' she said as she searched the seats. But apart from Ada, the bus was empty. Shirley screamed, hands to mouth in horror, 'My God, we've lost him!'

Mick switched off the engine and jumped out of his seat. 'Don't be bloody stupid. We can't have lost him.' He left niceties behind. 'Didn't yer bloody count heads?

Both women were aghast. 'We thought they were all on board. I don't think I counted – did you?' Panic was beginning to set in.

'Ah well, if you'd a listened to me,' crooned Ada, with, it must be said, a hint of satisfaction in her voice, 'I been trying all the way 'ome to tell yer we lost 'im.'

The Year of the Bull

'Andy the Bull. Yeah. Somehow he got called Andy,' Cliff reminisced. 'Not sure where that came from, since his official title was Kingsvale Linfield. Anyway, to all of us kids 1958 was the Year of the Bull.

'I remember the night Dad decided, with a slap of the *Jersey Journal* on his knee, to buy the bloomin' thing. Mum got such a shock she dropped her knitting needle as he bellowed out, "Pearl! We're gonna buy a bull."

'"What do you mean, dear?" said Mum as she bent to pick up the needle.

'"Waddya think I mean, luv – we need to put some new blood into this little herd of ours and I reckon this is just the boy – advertised right 'ere in the paper and not a bad price too."

'"But we've always used our own little bulls – they've done all right for us," Pearl queried, "and really, Arnold, can we afford to waste our small surplus when we don't really need to."

'"That's just me point." Dad rose from the chair, in his excitement pushing aside the leg of pork hanging to cure from above the doorway. He had the bull by the horns, so to speak. "Right now, we can afford to do it but who knows what the cream prices will be like next year and maybe it mightn't be only pigs and cream – we might even decide to take up a milk quota by then. The population's growing apace with all these townies comin' 'ere to settle."

'Dad would not be fobbed off by any of Mum's arguments and headed for the phone. We kids looked at each other in awe, shocked to silence at the sound of the handle winding and then Dad's loud voice.

'"Arnold Kerr 'ere. Ringin' about yer bull."

'Mum continued to knit, lips tight and looked at none of us.

'So the place was full of energy for the next few weeks. Dad seemed to whistle us earlier than usual to help with the cows – his wake-up call would sear through our brains – well, me brother Dennis, two years older, and me. I never though it was fair I had to do it when Merryl and Phillip got out of most things, them being a bit younger. It seemed they never did get to be old enough. It was always Dennis and me.

'"Come on, you kids, get down 'ere smart and feed these cows," he'd yell from the dairy, and we'd tumble out of bed, drag on a shirt and shorts and dash barefoot down the slope.

'Sometimes we'd pass Mum, coming up after milking to get breakfast, on the way and she'd often call back, "Don't be too hard on them, Arn, they're only little uns yet."

'Usually it was a rush to clean up the mess: wipe the machines, scoop up the shit, wash down the concrete and put out the feed, before dashing back to get dressed for school. We bolted down our Weetbix and if we were lucky, and Mum had had time to cook us some bacon and eggs, we hoed into those too. Grabbed bags and lunch boxes and off on the three mile hike to the bus. Sonter's bus stopped at the end of North Branch Road where about ten kids from local farms would wait and often, in winter, huddle around a small fire we'd build to keep warm. Our family had the longest walk as we lived right at the end of the valley, and though we pestered him, Dad would never let us ride. Reckoned we needed the exercise if we were sitting on our bums all day in class.

'But when the bull arrived, we were allowed to have the day off school. Everybody was excited – even Mr McKey, the headmaster. The arrival of a stud bull in our small community was quite an event.

'We'd been up early, done our chores without complainin', got the yard all shipshape and Mum even put on her good dress. Our pet magpie, Maggie, flew from one shoulder to another seeming to realise something was up as we hung about waiting for old Artie Smith to come down the road. He was picking up the bull from Kendall Station in his treasured Fargo – had a decent cage on it, big enough for a good sized animal.

'"Where the hell is he?" complained Dad, but no sooner said than Dennis shouted, "'ere he comes."

'And we could all see the tell tale cloud of dust rising way back down the road.

'"Geez, 'e's a nice-lookin' fella." Dad had a great beam of pride on his face, when we finally and carefully got him off the truck, down the race and into the yard.

'We'd all been holding our breath waiting for some mishap or show of fire from the mighty Kingsvale Lindfield. But he seemed docile enough, if slightly baffled, as he tucked into the bale of hay.

'"Yeah, I reckon you done a good deal there," agreed Artie. "You should've seen 'im stepping out of the cattle truck and being led down the station to me ute. Looked like a king, 'e did."

'Mum made tea and we all sat eating scones on the veranda but suddenly, as we relaxed looking with pleasure at our new acquisition, there was a fearful yell from Dad.

'"Christ," he exploded, "who took the bloody wire off the bale?" His eyes searched our faces, blank and uncomprehending. "Dennis? Cliff?"

'At our joint head shakes, he was down the steps like a madman. Didn't even pull on his boots.

'"Come on," he screamed. "We gotta find the wire."

'The wire? Hay bales were held together by wire in those days, which if eaten were likely to rip out a beast's guts.

'"Oh! God," we sinners all prayed, "let us find the wire." The panic spread – we searched every possible nook and cranny in a frenzy, but not a skerrick was found.

'Dad was out of his mind. '"He's eaten it, he's bloody eaten it – the vet, the vet," we heard as he scrambled back to the house.

'Well, the vet was called – the nearest was young Greg Coleman in Taree – late in the afternoon by now, and as the shadows lengthened we finally saw him bumping along the road in his little car.

'Mum jostled us kids back to the house – she didn't, nor did we, want to see what would happen next but in due course the details emerged.

'The vet had to anaesthetise the bull, who sank in the remains of the hay with a heavy thud, and then went to work. Slit the poor beast open and apparently searched through every organ and exit possible before declaring he could find nothing. He got to work with a sigh, sewed him up (did a neat job according to old Artie) straightened up, wiped himself with a rag, gave some rehabilitation instructions, said he'd send the bill and loped back to his car.

'Old Artie mumbled something like, "Gotta go – the missus will be wondering," and Dad spent the night in tears beside his prized possession.

'Next day at school our fame was a little less subdued than it might have been, and it was some while before visitors could come and see the heroic beast. But it must be said that, after three months convalescing with greater attention than in the local hospital, Andy, as he became known, was allowed to meet his pretty princesses. Over the years, he more than proved his worth but I never heard how much the vet had charged. Whatever, that was the last time Dad ever made such a momentous decision. Oh! And by the way, we never did find the wire. That was the greatest mystery.'

First Prize

Fullbull out of Bullbull owed his distinguished title to Jimmy, who was swinging on the farm gate the day Dad brought their first bull home. Scrambling off the top bar as the old truck, borrowed from Darce down the road, creaked up the hill to the yards, he took a flying leap onto the running board, poked his scruffy head in through the window and cried, 'Jwanna 'and?'

'Christ, kid, take it easy – yer'll kill us all before I can git the flamin' thing inter the paddick. Get off there and find yer mother.'

'Ma! Ma! The bull's 'ere,' Jimmy screeched toward the house. 'Yer gotta come 'n 'elp, the bull's 'ere.'

But before he reached the concrete step, Ma emerged wiping her hands on a grimy apron. The broken fly screen slammed behind her as Dad slowly braked the other side of the hay bales.

Jimmy was dancing, skinny legs springing from one bare foot to another, a melon grin and eyes enthralled. 'Cripes, e's a beaut, Dad. Jeez, 'e is. Got a bloody full belly, though,' he hooted, peeping through the wooden slats of the trailer. ''ello, old fella, ''ello, you old full bull.'

Fullbull – and so he was named.

The difficulties, without a loading ramp, without a race, of offloading a huge unfriendly beast already snorting and blowing at Jimmy, suddenly confronted them like a flooded river crossing. Dad looked at Ma. Ma wrung her hands on her apron again and Jimmy shut up. In the background, the house loomed friendly; despite peeling paint and the hole in the fibro due to a slight mishap with the tractor, right this moment it seemed a place of comfort.

Dad waved a dirty rag across his bald pate, replaced the greasy hat, mumbled, ''ow 'bout a cuppa?' and trundled inside.

I never heard how they got the bull into the yards. There was something about the hay bales being a mangled mess and Jimmy limping to school with a bandaged foot. Yes, and Darce down the road did let slip about the back tyre of the trailer being ripped to pieces, but, well, nobody cares about that any more, especially not Dad, whose pride runneth over, as last week he collected first prize in the local show.

Yeah, first prize. For the bull with the biggest balls.

A Slip of the Thumb

I hate mobile phones. As I see it, they are an antisocial invention that puts an end to ordinary, honest communication so that the masses can escape into the world of make-believe. It is rudeness personified when at a quiet dinner for four, in the middle of the host's favourite joke, a muffled but insistent jingle interrupts the table talk. The offending owner jumps to his feet to take the call (probably from the local SES wanting money) withdrawing from the pleasant situation leaving mine host open-mouthed mid-sentence. Really! I ask you.

Not for me. I've used an ordinary telephone all my life and see no need to be hampered by this extracurricular toy. However, pressure from the family mounted.

'But you should have one, Mum.' My daughter was firm. 'You never know when you might need it.'

'Yeah, Gran, what if you break down in the bush?' chirped my twelve-year-old grandson, waiting desperately for his thirteenth birthday to arrive, when (as a responsible teenager!) he will be rewarded with his own iPhone.

'I'd probably be out of range and have to change the wheel myself,' I retorted.

'Well, I think I've got my old work one somewhere, so why don't you try it and see how you go?'

My daughter did a house search and came up with a relatively basic model which served its purpose for some years until it finally gave up the ghost. Probably died from lack of use as it resided in my handbag, just in case, but there rarely was a just in case.

Still, I supposed I ought to get a replacement now that I was in the habit of carrying this disaster prevention aid, and I finally found a simple no-frills model that I thought I could handle. No camera, no GPS, no email. Just something to make a call. Unfortunately, even this tool for fools had me baffled and I was on the point of chucking it in the bin, but after countless directives and soothing murmurings from my daughter, 'Be patient, Ma, it will come to you,' I finally got the hang of it. I even managed to learn the art of texting and, I have to say, I felt rather chuffed.

One day I noticed a new message that turned out to be from Mary Walker, an old school friend. Well, not a real buddy buddy, but one of the girls in my class. I was a bit surprised to hear from her but everybody these days seems to be catching up on Facebook and LinkedIn. Cyberspace is overtaking our lives. I didn't mind hearing Mary's news, though I wondered about dementia, as her memory for names was pretty bad. And there was no reaction when I mentioned our Wells Grammar thirtieth class reunion, even though I'd found her in our group photo of the year of '52. Guess my mind isn't the greatest these days, so I can't be too critical.

Must say I'm not too fussed about the jokes she passed on – some of them were a bit much and I call myself pretty broad-minded.

Bet u luv this, she texted. An inane joke not worth a reply.

I remember her being a bit mousy at school but I guess we all change once we free ourselves from the confines of youth. She's had three husbands, she told me, and out looking for number four. Heavens, I'm too old for that caper but good luck to her. Funny, though, I don't remember hearing of Mary getting married.

'Just shows you don't know every bit of gossip,' my husband Wal observed from inside his newspaper.

Then came a message that had me baffled: *Remember bali? wow let's do it again.*

Do what? I replied.

Ha ha, she wrote back.

Ha ha what? Now I am getting puzzled. Bali was never one of my desired destinations.

U cant have forgotten brian, she texted.

Brian? Brian who?

Where r u at? cum on

What's going on? I pondered on who I could confide in over this latest text but it was getting a bit embarrassing. And Brian? Funny that. I didn't know any Brians except for Wal, that is, as it's really his first name. He was christened Brian Walter Hudson but always called Wally so as not to confuse him with his father Brian.

Bali?

Now that I think of it, Wal did have a stopover in Bali a couple of years ago coming home from seeing his family in England. Stayed at the Golden something or other. I didn't go because, well, you know how these family things are, they all get together and chitter-chatter about this memory and that event. No matter how they try to include you, it's always a bore, so why waste the money on another air fare. He didn't have much to say about Bali when he got back. Mumbled it was all right – overrated. I agreed with him, so didn't press for details but…

I texted Mary. *What hotel did we stay in?*

Where's yr brain – golden delight of course.

Date?

Wots got in 2 u sept 2010.

September – shoulder time, cheaper fares. Anger was mounting. Too many things were matching up. My insides were sizzling. It was nearly impossible to text I was shaking so much.

What school did you go to?

You barmy – forgotten blackie high.

My breath got caught in my throat – I thought I was going to choke or be sick. I needed air, ran outside, vaguely heard the loud bang of the broken screen door. My world was suddenly exploding – now I understood what it means when they say it feels like a bad dream. A million thoughts crazed my brain. Who was this woman? Certainly not an old school friend. Though one with the same name. What kind of orgy was it? Sex party. A joyful threesome? Wal and I hadn't had sex for years. Said he couldn't do it any more, though heavens above I'd tried hard enough. So what was his part in this nightmare? A picture of his flabby, naked body, paunchy stomach and skinny legs entangled with smooth young limbs was not a pretty one. Even less pretty was the memory of the time I bought this sexy nightgown in the hope of spicing up the bedroom. How embarrassing was that? He just turned away, muffled into the pillow something like 'Not your style, Sal.'

Somehow, thoughts became irrelevant. What was relevant was the fact that in five minutes flat a small, black, hand-held piece of modern technology had betrayed secrets never meant to be discovered. It had exposed the inadequacies of my averagely happy, comfortable, ordinary marriage and with a furious yell I savagely slammed that rotten mobile on the concrete drive. Bits and pieces flew in all directions, with black plastic, wires, batteries, littering the ground. Ruined beyond repair. Just like my fifty-two-year-old relationship.

There must be a reason why I had such a passionate hate of mobile phones. Now I knew what it was.

Central Station: A Twofold Tale

Eleisha couldn't believe it would be so cold even though it was winter, and Central Station, its bare heartless self, only added to her discomfort. She'd never been there but heard about it from Aunty Sal, who painted a far pleasanter picture of Sydney's major train hub. If she'd had a coat or jumper of any sort, she might not have felt the draughty chill so badly, but at home she could do without. Winter in the tropics is mild and none of her mob had a jacket to lend even if she had thought of it. Her body needed the toilet in this miserable weather.

'Gotta go an' have a pee,' she shivered to Ned. 'Wait here. I won't be long.'

Ned was cold too and wishing he was still back home. He felt agitated by the crowd swirling past like a vast uncontrollable flood. A silent distracted field of faces searching for…he couldn't guess what. But he had to do it, to come with El. The job had fallen to them and the journey had to be made. He blamed poor old Aunty Sal for sending them south. Blamed her for dying. Well, not so much for dying, though she could have left off the grog a bit, but for wanting her ashes thrown into the sea from the rocks at Bondi. Why she'd want that when they really belonged in the rainforest he didn't know. There was a secret story about those rocks at Bondi but nobody would tell it – he pleaded with Dan to know the reason.

'You just gotta go, boy, you just gotta go. That's what Aunty Sal wanted and she's family. We do it for 'er.'

It had been a nightmare – travelling for days with little packets of food.

'Can't waste money we ain't got.' Eleisha had prepared. They had plastic bags with sandwiches that soon became a mash, mangoes that leaked their juices through the crumbling biscuits and cheese that smelled like dead dog.

He felt embarrassed by the looks of the other passengers as El fished in this bag or that for the next nibble. He could feel their whispers, their critical eyes. She'd insisted on bringing her pillow (getting grubbier by the day) to endure the long nights as the train rattled and swayed, grimly, purposefully, from one state to the next. And the ashes of course. He was reminded to look under the seat, making sure the green Coles bag containing the box was still there. Handles securely tied with blue rope.

'Can't believe ashes could be so 'eavy,' Eleisha grumbled. ''spose it's bones and all.'

'Reckon it's nothing but bones – everything else would've gone up in smoke. Might find some false teeth or gold fillings, though.'

'I was told they always take 'em out first but dunno when they'd get the chance to do it.'

'Well, there wasn't much else left of the old girl – 'spose they burnt the coffin too.'

'Shocking waste if they did. Do yer reckon that's why it's so 'eavy?'

Ned was unable to answer. It was too close to the bone, so to speak, for him. He couldn't believe he would ever be dead. How do you understand the concept of not being? Not waking to the sunrise, feeling the soft rain, listening to the birds, diving under a wave, throwing stones. Spirits are all very well but you can't touch a spirit, or kick the footy with a spirit, or feel the soft breasts of a spirit. Nah. Something not to think about. Except, of course, the death of Aunty Sal had made them all think about it. And what happens afterwards. But Ned didn't want to learn about these things. Didn't want to know that there'd be a time when there isn't an anymore.

Eleisha thankfully came into focus allowing Ned to get on with being in the here and now as she led him through the archway to the street, 'There must be a bus to Bondi somewhere outside this dump.'

*

Carl had been searching for food. Central wasn't too bad if you got in before the others – bins often contained uneaten chips, leftover hamburger pieces, pie crusts, and not so long ago he'd found nearly half a chicken. But this morning there was nothing. He'd missed out. The garbage truck must have been early. He felt hopeless and useless – unable to provide anything for them.

Why had he been so stupid? Allowed this to happen. Let Jen persuade him they should move to the city. She was so excited about it – they'd both be able to get jobs, afford their own flat, go dancing, have fun. And most important of all be free of the restrictions of living in a small country town. When Jen twined her arms around his neck and looked into his eyes with such guile, he was a lost cause. How could he resist? He didn't – though their parents had fought against it. Put every possible obstacle in the way. But what Jen wants, Jen knows how to get. Except that it hadn't worked out as she planned. No jobs. No flat. Savings gone leaving them practically starving. And both too proud to go home.

Of the two, Carl felt their failure most. He was tired, defeated, humiliated. The effort to face the truth of their fiasco, that he was now one of the thousands of homeless that he would once have only vaguely recognised, was more difficult than plodding the streets or queuing at the soup kitchens. And it had been his fault, lining up for a job at the laundry, that they were late last night missing out on the Friday Freebies, as it was called, at St John's church. Nearly all the food was gone when they got there. They shared the scrapings from the saucepan of soup with apologies from kindly volunteers. 'You got to be in early,' they all said sympathetically.

He leant against the last empty bin numb at the thought of going back to Jen, left huddled in the station wagon, empty-handed. Last night had been freezing and seemed colder on empty bellies. Her soft weeping lulled them to sleep in the end, but he had to be awake early to move the car from its no parking zone and then head off in search for food. Tearfully, he stared around the dreary platform, his mind unable to outwit the circumstances. He could throw himself in front of a train, that would solve the problem. Jen would be all right – she'd have the car. And she would find another bloke much better than him. But then, as quickly as the thought came to him, it left, for his brooding eyes had zoomed in onto a green Coles supermarket bag.

It was half under one of the seats where a fellow sat waiting, in a bit of a daydream it seemed to Carl. Immediately his body went into action. It hardly took a minute for him, with practised zeal, to slither up, catlike, and silently, smoothly, slide the bag out from under the station bench. Excitement tickled his chest and with a smug smile he nonchalantly made for the exit.

He pictured Jen's delight and surprise when she saw his offering and felt her gentle arms around his neck, her lips on his as words mingled with kisses. 'A supermarket bag full, you're a genius. How did you do it?'

Filled with new energy, he could hardly wait to explore its contents and once outside the station moved fast enough not to notice the dreary morning and the cold grey constriction of the wretched streets.

*

Ned and Eleisha alighted at a vacant-looking Bondi. Not the usual postcard picture at all. A dull, depressing sky hung above sullen waves and a brisk nor'-easter pestered their inadequate clothing. There was not a person on the beach. A soulless day in a concrete jungle. So bleak.

Ned stared towards the spray drenching the rocks but felt strangely overcome by an inexplicable chill as he gazed at the seas relentless motion. 'Why here?' he wondered aloud.

'Long story,' was Eleisha's rather abrasive reply. 'The only thing I'll say is it's all about a kid.'

There was a bitterness in her voice but she jutted her chin and chivvied them along, leaving Ned more in the dark than ever. Better start for the south rocks, no time to hang about if they were going to get the midday train back north. Head bent into the wind, Eleisha pictured her lost cousin, Aunty Sal's secret – a blonde, blue-eyed, dark-skinned little girl. Only lived to be three years old when she was washed off the rocks while fishing with her drunken father.

'Is the bag too heavy for you, Ned? Want me to have a go?' she turned to him enquiring.

The bag?

Never in all his life had Ned felt the ground drop and heave from under him like it did at this moment. Never had he longed so deeply to belong in another place. Though he instantly knew he was to blame his reaction was to pass the buck.

'The bag? Haven't you got it?'

'Course I haven't. You know I left it with you when I went to the loo.'

He was speechless with disbelief, she speechless with rage. Her whole body quivered. A bubbling volcano ready to erupt. He felt her anger like molten lava about to engulf him.

'You stupid, useless, fuckin' idiot,' she choked, 'Oh God. Oh God. How could you?'

*

It didn't happen as Carl had anticipated. So often dreams change, he had learned, before they become a reality. He found it difficult to waken Jen curled under a pile of blankets and had to knock several times, hard, on the car window, before she lifted her tear-stained, dishevelled head to look blankly at him. She seemed disconnected.

'Open the window,' he called. 'I've got us some food.' He lifted the bag for her to see but his enthusiasm was met with morose immobility. 'Open up and we'll see what's inside – I haven't looked. I waited to share it with you. How would you like some juicy apples or oranges?' he cajoled.

Silently she wound down the window, let him drop the bag inside while he unlocked the door and climbed over the seat. 'It's so cold,' she grumbled. 'Where did you get it?'

'Don't worry about that. Just let's see what we've got – I bet you'll never guess what's in there.'

Her numbed fingers struggled with the knotted blue rope.

'Here,' he leant over in his urgency, 'let me do it.' He fiddled impatiently and at last, 'There we go, open sesame.'

Slowly she pulled out wads of newspaper. They seemed to protect something. She looked at him accusingly. Then lifted out an ungainly long shaped something or other wrapped in an old, stained, red checked tea towel. It was so heavy she could hardly hold it up – she strained but let it fall. Ned's excitement had evaporated. Concern took its place followed by a horrible sinking in the guts. What on earth…? An opaque bluish plastic container lay between them on the scrambled blankets. Impossible to see through, they stared at it with some foreboding. Was it a bomb?

Jen shrank back shocked, eyes squeezed shut, wrist in mouth, as he carefully lifted it, surprised by the weight which he hadn't noticed before. Sweaty now, his heart beat overtime as he shook it. Gingerly at first then harder from side to side. All they heard was the sound of something like sand being blown in the wind. Or waves splashing on the shore.

Jen opened her eyes. They widened, deep, black, filled with comprehension and an intense contempt. So contemptuous he recoiled as if slapped on the cheek. And looked, as she wordlessly, shakingly, pointed. A sticker, attached on one side, told the story.

Everglades Crematorium – Salaisha Rae Pintintkara
b. 21.4.1950 d. 4.08.2013
No. 1900659

He was mute with disbelief. Mind said it can't be true. Fact told him otherwise. Incredulously, furiously, he punched the container while a movie playback of her sauntering off, shrugging, turning her back without a glance, tracked across his brain. The harder he tried, the more it resisted. Even the lid was impossible to dislodge until he attacked it with his penknife. Then, like a burst pipe, it flew open, spraying a greyish sandy powder all over the blankets – a pea soup fog descended wrapping a cloying grit around them.

Jen screamed, dusting the stuff off as if it were stinging green ants and scrambled over into the front of the car. 'You stupid, useless, fuckin', idiot…' she choked. 'Oh God. Oh God. How could you?'

Sarsaparilla Supermarket

(a Patrick White parody)

Lassie Hogson checked in front of the cluttered window trying to see through Christmas greetings, though it was over weeks ago. But couldn't. Only the top of her spruce head reflected behind the podgy snowman and seductive ads. 'Mini Meals. 2 for 9c.'

She did, in fact, pat her head, smugly, while searching to remember the price of four-ounce spaghetti at Rooks down the road.

Then wondered, 'Do you like spaghetti?'

The small girl longed for 'Raspberry pigs – 3 for 20c'. But was absent-mindedly sucking her skinny plait. With the blue checked ribbon.

'What?'

'Spaghetti. With cheese and tomato sauce. For lunch?'

'I don't know.'

'But you like it?'

'Do I?'

'Well, don't you?'

'I s'pose so.' Flat. And stared at her wet plait. Flipped it to right and left. It jumped like it was electrocuted.

'Really, Moppet! Just to find something you like for lunch. Heavens, when I was your age I was never asked just ate what was put in front of me not all these ice creams and sweets you kids get nowadays without a thank you or… 'Moppet! Moppet!'

'May-LEEN!' And called to the disgruntled figure off down the street, skinny legs passing the butcher's by now, dodging that rude Bud Slate from Murdock Street on his bike slouched over the handlebars sucking delight from the bottom of a large Whisky & Walnut.

At last inside, when she had neatly wriggled through the chrome turntable and marshalled the stubborn trolley to clatter, amongst the Cut Prices, Weekly Specials, Sarsaparilla Specials that dazzled, Lassie Hogson took a deep breath. But she did not venture on. Not then. Her thoughts were not tidy yet. But heard.

''Ello, Glad. Gawd, it's hot. How's things?' Sloppily Lola pushed. In rubber thongs. 'Jeez, them termarters expensive. Just lookit that! Four lousy termarters for forty cents.'

'Hello, Lola.' Gladys heavily descended to the Slimmits that leered from the bottom shelf. Held her stomach and stretched. Looking pathetic. 'It's hot, all right. I feel like a sack. Whenever will it rain?'

'Don't worry, luv, it's gotta be over soon, the Lord'll bless us when 'e's ready so…morning, Mrs Hogson.'

Lassie ignored. But constructed a smile for Gladys, whom she liked. And was startled then by the squeaking. It was Moppet flying past Detergents and Health & Beauty Aids with Mrs Doyle's Beetrice trailing dodging customers.

'MAYLEEN – BEETRICE,' calling to stop.

But the 'Special Assorted Biscuits limit 2' smiling on their cardboard stand, crackled and fell, skated with ease except Beetrice stepped, slithered dumbly among their cellophane and crumbs. Then the flour, the sugar, the Doggie Food toppled and the prim salt soldiers, the vinegar that might crack…until her mother leant to grab and haul and puff past Marj at the checkout onto the pavement away from stifled laughter. Mortified.

'What on earth do you think you're doing, my lady, behaving like a little hooligan?' Lassie Hogson screamed between clenched teeth. 'Look at your dress. Just wait till your father hears…whatever's got into you these holidays?'

Moppet could have told her about Beetrice's guinea pig. Soft and silvery. But didn't. Besides she said, 'Where's me spaghetti?'

What Is Love?

From all I'd heard, it was a ridiculous decision. Imagine a woman of her age marrying him. A sedate lady of English descent and an islander who had somehow managed to sneak into the country without papers. He had no work; she owned a bookshop.

How could she? Of course he had everything to gain. Let's face it, in another ten years she'd probably be dead and he'd be sitting pretty. In the meantime, he'd got what he wanted – the right to live in the country of his choice. But what on earth could she hope to get out of it? And she was old enough to be his mother.

All her friends loathed him. A dreadful man, they said.

He was what he was. A native islander born to the beach, who played the languid life of sun and sand; lazy beyond belief, illiterate and irresponsible but obviously not stupid, they had to admit. The way he managed to snare their special friend, and despite advice from everyone, they just turned up in the shop one day and said they were married. Apparently nobody believed them at first – didn't know whether to laugh or cry, or what.

About six months later, two young men arrived on the scene. Some relatives or other of his. They seemed quite at home in the neat white bungalow and fortunately soon went off to work – somewhere – though they hardly spoke a word of English. Dark, tight curls and smooth brown skin, like the husband, they loped along as if they had all the time in the world, their beautiful white smiles, for some reason, aggravating her friends intensely.

To make it worse, only a little while after, three younger girls were added to the family. These happy children were sent to school, where they laughed all day and learnt practically nothing. Needless to say, at this stage the household was forced to move. They found a farm not far from town; a few acres protecting a decaying old house. Its sinking foundations and broken windows were eventually repaired, and the place became sort of liveable – as long as you didn't mind a walk to the loo, negotiating missing floorboards and sewing by kero lamps.

It was about this time I began working at the shop. The Come By Chance Bookshop. And had my life changed by meeting Mrs Tukefula. Her knowledge of books and authors was brilliant; she seemed to know every title and publisher in print and she always managed to have in stock just the book the customer wanted. She had a sixth sense in ordering and no rep ever tried to 'sell' to her. She knew (and they knew she knew) exactly what was needed. For me, who loved books, writing, reading, it was the perfect job and we had a perfect relationship. And that was only what the world could see. It was the inside – the 'she and I together in the same space pleasure' – that has stayed with me always.

The only issue was him. Mr Tukefula. Because she decided to give him an occupation. To everyone's dismay, she made him manager of her small firm.

Oh, how dapper he looked out of shorts and thongs and into crisp white shirts, trousers, clean shoes and socks. And 'dapper' to him meant control. He was king of the roost, having leapt from island beaches to managerial duties, and he implemented his wild ideas with gusto. Wild ideas that made the business tremble even sooner than the sceptics forecast. And plunged them into debt.

Why, oh why, I cried to myself home at night after another day of disasters. But for her own reasons she made no attempt to curb his fancies, was never critical, always patient and protective. What is love, I wondered.

Perhaps I understood a little, as they were kind to me who was living alone, and often invited me to the farm for tea. I always drove home feeling soft and contented, though I hardly knew why. Perhaps the happy atmosphere in that beat-up old place rubbed off on me a little. Made me wonder at my own unfortunate break-up. Always there would be tinkling laughter and smiling faces. The gentle boys teased the girls politely and the girls reacted uproariously. There seemed to be so many of them, I could never remember who was who and then his sister with baby, adding another dimension to the ménage.

In the kitchen, the old fuel stove was continuously stoked and wheedled while a huge roast spluttered oozing glorious juices. The smell of taos, blackberry pies and thick cream mingled with home-made alcoholic brews, mostly kava, that could have been half the reason for my contentment.

Not long after I had moved interstate, I was sad (though of course not surprised) to hear that the business had finally folded and even sadder when the news of her illness reached me. Somehow something rang a bell. Was that why she so coddled him? Had she been aware of her cancer for a long while? I would never know, because she had little time left and I hurried to her bedside for a final farewell. I prepared myself for a wretched visit as I heard the place was a shambles and that she was in a miserable state. I hated the thought that such an ill person could be cared for so unprofessionally, particularly as he was supposedly just as hopeless as head of the family as he had been in business.

I shouldn't have been surprised to see them all just as before, a little older, but still with the same shining faces, as if nothing was terribly amiss. Mr Tukefula held out his arms to me with his usual buoyant smile and led me into her room. She looked deathly but quite peaceful and very content to have his strong shoulder near. The room was smiling with a bright patchwork quilt, rose-coloured curtains and a bowl of autumn leaves beside her bed. Professional care, I thought, could not compare with this comforting togetherness.

When I rose to leav,e she reached our her poor hand. And smiled. It was for all of us there.

'You know, dear, I never dreamed this marriage could have brought me such happiness… Whatever they may say, he has given me a most wonderful family.'

What is love? By chance, the Come By Chance Bookshop had given me a little insight into the real joys of loving.

The Transaction

I was just fourteen when Charlie Croft came to town. I didn't speak
to him for more than a week after he arrived, didn't have the nerve, I
guess. With all the talk about him having this big property down south
and his fancy clothes, he wouldn't be interested in a kid like me. Still,
I used to see him often enough, mostly when I was riding home from
school. He'd be propping up a post down Main Street talking to the
fellas, and all the girls would be hanging around giggling. Gee, they
sure dressed smart since Charlie came to town. Yes, he was popular
all right. And generous too. Everybody knew it was drinks on him at
O'Mara's and there was always a zac or two for us kids.

'Get us a packet of fags,' he'd say, 'and yer can keep the change.'

I finally met him the day I dropped the bread. It went flying into
the gutter as I jumped up onto Bluey, and Charlie was the one to pick
it up. All of a sudden, I couldn't think of anything to say so I just sat
there holding the squashed loaf.

'What's yer name, kid?' he asked.

'Dummy,' I said, 'Dummy Jackson.'

'Dummy? Why Dummy?'

'I don't talk much,' I told him, staring at my dirty shirt.

'But what's yer real name.'

'John, I reckon.'

'Then I'm going to call you John. Might have a spare zac, John,
if you're round this way again.' And he strolled off down to meet the
mob.

I still remember how excited I was, and galloped wildly home. Ma
grumbled over the squashed bread but I hardly heard her.

I got my sixpence, I got it next day all right, and every day from then on. I seemed to be a kind of favourite of his, which made the other kids jealous. I was the centre of attention for once in my life and I thought Charlie was marvellous.

Out of the blue one day, he said, 'When am I going to meet yer folks, John?'

I didn't know what to say so I just said, 'Temorrer. Come to tea.'

I thought Dad would belt me when he heard but I got a surprise to see how pleased he was.

'Well, that'll be nice a visitor from down south. Lots of dough, I hear. Do us good to have some company. Go on now, boy, git and clean those bridles.'

All Mum said was 'I don't know how 'e'll like corned beef and cabbage but that's all 'e'll get unless the chooks do some layin.'

Charlie certainly won Ma and Dad over. I'd never seen Dad so taken before. He even got out the old bottle of rum he kept hidden in the cupboard behind the raincoats, and Charlie reckoned it was really fine stuff. And he told Ma he hadn't had a better feed since he left Sydney. Ma was looking more dolled up than usual and I could see she was happy to have a bit of a pat on the back. She had on a clean dress too, though it was torn under the arm and she still seemed to have a stale smell about her, and she'd even, as she called it, 'put her hair up'.

'Now get along, kid, get to your chores. Charlie and me's going to have a little chat,' Dad said as Ma cleared away the dishes.

So I strolled outside to feed the chooks and the cows, then I'd go and have a chat with Bluey.

I certainly loved that bloomin' horse, more than anything – or anybody for that matter. If I wasn't riding her, I was out in the shed feeding and grooming, stroking and talking or just being with her. I was about ten when old Jack Smith on the farm over the way died. The foal, a little runt of a thing was left behind so I brought her home and nobody seemed to care – except Dad. Said what was I goin' ter feed 'er on, we had nothing to spare for stray 'orses. But I got a job with Bert McQuilley the baker on Saturday mornings, and that helped to buy some oats.

'Better get rid of the thing,' Dad had said, 'or she'll send us broke.'

But I had looked after her no problem.

In the middle of my thinking, I heard the sound of a sulky rattling down the lane and ran to see what was happening. Dad and Charlie had obviously hitched up Bluey while I was in the cow paddock and were driving off along the road.

'What are they doing, where are they going?' I yelled at Ma in the kitchen.

'Takin' Charlie back to town.'

'But he didn't even say goodbye.'

'Well, maybe 'e was worried you'd blow a fuse.'

'Why would I blow a fuse?' Suddenly a fearful feeling spread over my body. I knew something bad was happening.

'Maybe it's because 'e sold yer 'orse.

'What horse? Bluey? He can't. She's not his to sell.'

She told me the men had started talking; Charlie said he had a solid little business in mind if only he had a decent kind of horse. Course, he didn't have any ready cash but had a block of land down south, been in the family for years, that he could do a deal with. Little gold mine, actually, he said – fertile soil, good water – could grow a nice little herd there.

'Well, yer can 'ave the kid's 'orse if yer want – solid little mare and a real 'ard worker, yer father said, so they went off into town to sign some papers. Sounds like yer father's goin' ter own a bit of land down south.'

I must have lost my block then – it's a long while ago now - but I remember screaming round the yard and running into the fowl pen and kicking all the poor chooks out, flapping and clucking, and into the cow yard, and let all the cows out and kicked and hit and they fussed and clattered, and poor Lottie the sow tried to protect her piglets from my crazy rage till I fell on the ground and sobbed and sobbed.

Tears stopped hatred replaced them. I got up, went into the house, collected some gear, took all the money out of the jar on Dad's desk and left. I heard Ma shouting but I never turned my head. Never looked back.

I heard afterwards that Charlie Croft sold the horse, got twenty-five quid from Hugh Barnes on the old Mine Road. Sold her the very next day. Quit town and nobody heard of him since.

Work was hard to get, particularly for a kid my age, but I finally came across a shed boss while I was waiting on a railway siding. He was off to a job out west and said the cook needed some help. He'd take me on as slushy if I was prepared to work. How old was I anyway? 'Eighteen,' I lied, and he didn't believe me, but that was how I started in the sheds.

A slushy does all the dirty work, whatever it is, and I never stopped working all day. I chopped wood, lit the stove, got the milk and made the butter. I peeled spuds and I peeled onions and I washed up and I cleaned up. I kneaded dough and I peeled spuds and I chopped meat and I peeled onions. I peeled spuds and I washed up and made the tea and…and fell dead asleep on the ground by the fire. It was a terrible job and if I hadn't been so filled with hatred – if I hadn't hated Dad so much and Charlie, who I'd so admired – I'd have chucked it in pretty quick.

It was a fair while before I managed to get a job as junior rouseabout. It wasn't much of a step up but anything was better than peeling potatoes. The first shed wasn't too bad but, blimey, the next was hell. They couldn't get any boys at that time and three of us had to pick up for fifteen shearers. They were real mean brutes, that bunch. They never stopped swearing and yelling and you never knew which way to run.

You picked up the belly wool and you picked up the fleeces and threw to the wool rollers and then they yelled 'Tar' and you'd run with the pot and sweep up and clean up and tar from another and slop it and sweep up with two fleeces waiting to pick up and throw and pick up and throw. I was the slowest, and the worst, and got cursed the most.

I covered a fair bit of country over the next few years. I didn't take much notice of where we were or what the crew was like, and nobody took much notice of me. I went from junior rouse to senior, then to piece picker and wool roller, and got to know the shed routine pretty well.

I first met Gladys about this time; she was a barmaid who was also on the wander, pretty and popular out west, one of the few who bothered to talk to me. 'Come on, kid,' she'd say, 'drink up, life's not that bad,' and off she'd go to flirt with anyone else.

It was a good many years before I came near home again but I found out then that Ma had died not all that long after I'd left. She was found drowned in the local creek. There were apparently no suspicious circumstances and her death was classed as accidental but rumour had it she was broken-hearted after the disappearance of her only son. I relived that terrible day of my departure and found, rather than blaming myself, that I just refuelled my hatred of Dad. If he hadn't sold Bluey, Ma would be still be alive. It was his fault. Dad had sold the place and was living in town – taken to the booze, it seems, and using Charlie's land as credit wherever possible. My land, it should have been. But I'd get it one day. I would wait. That's what my life was all about – waiting to get back at my old man.

One spring we were doing a small job down south and I ended up sharing a room with an old fella called Mac Dermott. I never found out his real name. Everyone called him Mac and he was the only friend, apart from Bluey, I'd ever had. I don't know how we became friends. He used to talk away and if I didn't answer he didn't seem to mind.

One day, one Sunday it was, we were doing our washing outside the kitchen and he said, 'What's eatin' yer, kid? What's on yer mind?'

I didn't answer but just stared at the soap in my hand, frothing bubbles.

'Yer gunner tell me? It's best get it off yer chest.'

I let the trousers drop back in the bucket and flopped onto the grass. And then I told him. Slowly he nodded and understood. I never talked so much again but Mac gave me books to read and taught me to play crib, and how to make shoes out of sacking, strong and sturdy, and cut my hair, and I cut his. We must have looked a strange pair – a white-haired weather-beaten old man and a big silent kid.

I wanted to shear and said to Mac, 'I'll do yer washing for you if I can finish off yer sheep at the end of the run.'

'Yer don't have ter do me washing, kid. I'll be happy ter 'elp yer learn. And you can start a coupla minutes before the whistle blows as well.'

The engine started. I'd haul out Mac's first sheep and start on the belly. 'Keep 'is 'ead back, keep it outa yer road.' Then to the head. 'Not so close, boy, don't wanta skin the poor mug,' and the whistle would blow and Mac took over.

So before too long I started on the boards. Old Mac and I always stayed together – he'd go off on a break to the coast every so often but we'd catch up somewhere later on. He always came back with plenty of yarns but it was the old times that meant so much to him.

'By crikey, you blokes got it easy these days,' he'd say. 'Why, if you was shearing in the eighties, you'd have known a thing or two. It was tough in those days all right, but Jove we had some good times too. And the dances, they knew how to turn them on, specially at show time. There were a terrific lot of sheilas round in them days – sure knew how to make a fella feel good – oh! And did they dress up?' He would gaze into the fire as the memories danced into sight, a mug of tea held warmly in his hands.

And then Mac died.

'Didn't cha know 'e 'ad a dicky 'eart,' the blokes said. 'Poor mutt, didn't 'e ever tell yer? Ad it fer years. Knew 'e'd go at any time. But wasn't one ter sit 'ome and mope.'

The local ambulance had gone on call so we took his body into the town next day, eighty-five miles through the dust, and I sat in the back of the ute trying to hold him still. Make him comfortable even though he wouldn't feel a thing. But he slipped and slid and bumped out of my arms. The grey blanket came unwrapped and as his head fell sideways I realised how little hair he had left and how wrinkled his skin was.

Somehow I had never noticed. I picked up his arm to wrap him tight against the swarming flies and felt the soft hand, heavy – like dough. I was back being a slushy and making bread and I wanted to be sick.

I shouted to him over the rattling and jarring of the ute, 'Mac! Mac! Talk ter me. Talk ter me. I want yer back. You can't die. Why didn't yer tell me?' My tears mixed with dust, ran down his face as I held him in my arms. We rocked and moaned and cried across the miles to town.

They didn't have a coffin. They could get one in a couple of days but it was ninety-eight in the shade, so they dug a hole and dumped him in.

'…dust to dust, ashes to ashes…' the bush brother droned, swatting the flies with a stick.

Mac had no belongings to speak of – nobody knew of family – so I crammed his old hat on my head, collected my pay, climbed on board the mail truck and headed still further west. On and on. And the years passed. The heat came and went. Jobs came and went. Life came and went.

One day, waiting to change trains at a small siding, I met a tramp. He sat on his swag, hunched and staring, puffing a drooping cigarette.

'Do you know how long before the train comes, mate? I asked, as a peculiar sensation that something was familiar hit me.

Watery yellow eyes looked up.

'Blimey! Charley!' I cried excitedly. 'Charlie Croft. It is Charlie, isn't it?'

'Yes, it's Charley,' he grumbled. 'What's it to you, fella?'

'But I'm Dummy. You know. Dummy Jackson.'

'Can't say I do, fella,' he said, staring on.

'But you must. It's Dummy. You bought me horse. Bluey, the grey mare, and you sold it. You sold my horse. You remember. You must.'

'Can't say I do, fella. Now leave a man alone, can't yer.' He took another puff and turned away.

I realised in that instant what they mean about being struck dumb. I was gobsmacked. Totally unable to comprehend the situation.

Thoughts began to surface as I stood, still staring open-mouthed at the back of his hat. Is he lying? Acting? Or is he for real? Down and out and had it? Surely he couldn't have come to this? After all his tricks and fancies? Could he?

Numbly, speechless, I walked to the other end of the siding and sat down to wait while my fancies pictured my block of land, its fine pasture, good water and healthy cattle peacefully grazing.

I finally ended up as a station hand, one of many, on a quarter of a million square miles of mulga. It was hard work, hard and monotonous and lonely. I was used to my own company, so it suited me, and I stayed year after year. And year after year my hatred of Dad persisted. Year after year, I waited. Ben Shaw was a good boss, tough and no fancy manners, but we knew where we stood with him. He taught me a lot in my time out there, for you had to know a bit about everything if you were to survive in that kind of country.

I'd been with him a good while before he said, 'What's up, Dummy? No family to visit?'

'Nup,' I said.

'Too bad, but you ought to get away – we all need a break out here. Does you good to have a change, keeps you going for another year. What about the coast?'

'I'm okay,' I said. 'I'll just stick around.'

I think I was pretty well settled there for good when it finally happened. I still knew I had to have the land, out of habit, I suppose, more than anything else, and I still hated me Dad, though that was probably out of habit too. It was all so far away, and I had been waiting for so long, but when the letter came I knew what was in it.

'Looks like something interesting Dummy,' Ben Shaw said as he handed it to me. 'This what you've been waiting for?'

I didn't open the letter then, knowing what was in it. I somehow couldn't. It was later on that night as I leant against the veranda post smoking that it hit me. I felt as if the blood was shooting up my legs and my arms and into my head. I threw the cigarette away and rushed inside, feverishly tearing the letter open while bits of envelope flew everywhere. On the bunk, I smoothed the paper out.

The solicitors, Hamley & Wells, begged to inform me that as a beneficiary of the late P.R. Jackson, it would be to my advantage to contact them as soon as possible as certain details concerning transfer of property to my name must be supplied.

I stretched slowly and walked over to the cupboard, where my only grog, half a bottle of rum, was listlessly resting since its last use many months ago. I drank slowly, staring out the door into the twilight and then the darkness until the bottle was empty, thinking blankly of nothing until I eventually fell back on the bunk and slept.

When I reached town a few days later, I still felt drunk or woozy or out of it, but booked into the pub and was surprised to find Gladys serving behind the bar. I hadn't seen her for a long time or even heard of her whereabouts but she was looking as perky as ever and since I had to wait several days for a train we did quite a bit of catching up. I felt warm in her company, remembering the friendly way she had encouraged a shy young man so long ago. I must say, it didn't take her long, after she had heard my story, to convince me that we should get married.

'You know, Dum,' she had said, 'neither you or I are getting any younger and I reckon it'd be a damn good idea if we was to get hitched. Time you 'ad someone to look after you, and me too for that matter.'

I was pretty pleased with the idea and really didn't care if she was, as rumour had it, marrying me for my money. They reckoned she thought she was a bit smart to have grabbed a fella with heaps of dough and be able to move out of the west as well.

There were quite a few to see us off on the train headed for Sydney via Brisbane and a marriage celebrant.

Glad went crazy about the city. 'This is the life, darl.' she bubbled, 'Just look at them shoes, oh, and the furs. I just gotter have a fur and mink too. No more rabbit for me.'

She was happy to lie in bed in luxury the morning I set off to find the land. I was happy she did too, as this moment was to be for me, the best in my life, and something I really could not share. I selfishly wanted to hug the joy to myself.

It was about thirty miles out of town, the agent said as he drove us through the city, but I saw none of it. Factories, suburbs, outskirts passed by without my being aware of them. I sat back, eyes closed and smiling as I pictured the future. I could see it all. My home, my family, stud herd in neat fenced paddocks, prize ribbons hanging on the wall, and me, sitting in my leather armchair contentedly smoking my pipe. Look at me now, Dad. Just look at me now. You stole my greatest friend but in the end I won the prize.

'Well, I guess this as about as far as I can go, mate. Don't want to get bogged trying to get down there – your block should be just before that power line.'

I came out of my happy reverie to see the driver pointing to a muddy track and I looked across at a patch of desolate country. I lurched forward and sprang out of the car. 'What are you talking about? This isn't it. You must have taken the wrong road – my land is fertile river flats not this bit of junk.'

'Listen, mate, you said Arthur Street, Vineyard, and this is it, whether you like it or not. Your bit will be somewhere down there. It'll be marked somehow.' He pointed his thumb. 'You want to look or do we go back to town?'

Mechanically, I walked about a hundred yards through the wet scrubby weed until I came to a rotten, leaning post where an arrow pointed to my land. I felt like I felt when I saw poor Bluey disappearing from my life. Incomprehensible disbelief. It seemed as if I was somehow watching from a distance. Maybe I had been doing this for all those years; all my life, picturing the happy ending. I didn't feel my feet touching the ground or the water in my boots from splashing through puddles. My body was emptied. Its contents spilled on the swampy ground. Impossible to believe what I was seeing.

This little gold mine Charlie had so eloquently and enthusiastically described, this wonderful property down south, was no more than a few acres of dead, sour, useless scrubland. And to cap it off, huge pylons towered there, joined by heavy, sagging power lines that disappeared from sight over the little rise.

And I was standing in the mud, suddenly feeling the water in my boots, listening to a crazy old magpie sitting on those lines not far above my head. And I began to feel the ground beneath my feet again and I had a sense of lightness all over me, a sense of freedom. I wriggled my toes in my wet socks and I smiled and I felt good.

'Back to town,' I laughed at the surprised agent as I flopped my bedraggled, muddy, wet body into his pristine clean car.

I laughed and laughed for all the thirty miles. It wasn't as if I had lost something. It was as if I had won the lottery. I was free for the first time since I was fourteen. I was free of hatred and I was free from waiting. Life beckoned. Happiness tickled me all over.

Oh, but what about Glad!

The Shiralee

She knew as soon as she entered that the voices would subside, momentarily, as she made her way to the empty table at the back of the restaurant. She always had this effect. Her size alone would do it but the lavish blonde hair and red dress, long, low and flamboyant, were sure to cause a stir.

She eased her over-a-hundred-kilo body onto the table, settled a gold-sandalled foot with glistening toenails on the facing leather chair and sexily leant over her guitar. There wasn't one face not statue-like in anticipation. A few seconds' pause and she began to sing.

There was magic in the air whichever way you looked at it. The deep full voice flowed with the melody of the instrument, delighting the audience. Her upbeat songs urged them to dance, the dirty ditties seemed funnier than usual and the love songs made fingers touch. Those about to leave ordered more coffee and relaxed again while she strummed from Italy to Spain, folk or jazz, wartime and musical. Her songs made the foursome sparkle, the couples kinder, the singles sadder and the night inside the room began to glow kindled by the expertise of those fat, white fingers.

'Who is she?'

'Bettina La Mure.'

A mystery apart from her name. This was well known in the mountain village. She passed through occasionally, unexpectedly. Sometimes she stayed a few days, sometimes only a night. Apparently there was a child somewhere – a little girl.

For over an hour she played. And sipped. The rich red liquid glowed in the glass beside her. The young waiter took care that the level never fell and the music rushed stronger and faster. The clapping, the cheers, the foot beat. 'Tremendous', 'fantastic', 'more' and 'more' echoed across the tables. She heard, smiling sunlessly – half closed eyes and long false lashes disguising her thoughts.

Quite suddenly she stopped, drained the glass and graciously propelled herself towards the door. There was a sudden silence – the restaurant seemed empty and for moments the room was hushed. Then slowly people came to as if awakening and a lethargic move was made to pay bills and gather coats. The alpine night was cool although winter snows had not begun and a subdued atmosphere surrounded those wandering back to warm beds. The singer had left them with a strange melancholy that only settled after the buoyancy of her voice had faded into the night.

Back in the chalets, the word went around.

'Bettina's back.'

'Bettina?'

'Yes.'

'Here?'

*

Her real name was Betty. 'Bettina La Mure', her mother had ventured, was a bit much. What was wrong with her own good honest name? Betty didn't care for her good honest name nor for the woman who had christened her. She was contemptuous of her mother's struggle to provide for them both and even more so of those women who required her services in the their big brick homes.

'Why can't they get off their backsides and clean their own dirty stoves?' She'd slung out at the age of sixteen, fed up by her mother's constant admiration of her employers' latest luxury. 'I don't know how you can stand it. I'll never have any lazy bitch telling me to get down and clean her bloody lavatory. God! You might just as well be dead.'

'But Betty, it's…well, what else can I do? It's not unpleasant. And what about that jumper you're wearing and all the other things Mrs Buckingham has given us?'

'Chucked in the ragbag, you mean, and for heaven's sake don't call me Betty.'

The fly screen banged as she waded into the backyard – even as a teenager she was hugely overweight and strained to move quickly. Her awkward gait made it look as if she had wet her pants and Mrs Buckingham's old grey jumper wrinkled too tightly about her obese body. But the Blue Bird Café was only a few doors around the corner so she could choose the creamiest cream buns and wander back to the flat slowly stuffing her huge frame with more calories than her mother would consume in a month. Walking and thinking.

Remembering Mrs Howlett's time. The beautiful two-storey house in Violet Street where her mother went to work each day. Every morning, she hurried up the side path to the back door, through the laundry, where she hung her shabby coat and changed from her old shoes into even older ones. Betty longed for such a house. A red grapevine about the rough-hewn stone, lacy curtains whispering in the breeze and in the winter daffodils lining the path from the gate to the front veranda. Her young dreams hoped to replace the two-roomed flat behind the grocer's store where the lino was torn and greasy and everything was dreadfully second-hand. Her heart burned with envy.

Until the day she'd come home from school with a pain in the belly she could hardly take, and stopped at the Howletts' needing her mother.

Miss Hilda, the middle girl, and about her own age, had haughtily shut the front door. 'Round the back,' she ordered. 'Your mother's in the kitchen.'

Betty was sick on the petunias by the front porch. While she tried to wipe the spattered dress with her cardigan sleeve, a sudden loathing of her mother overwhelmed her. She went home alone, fiercely, a dry hatred in her mouth, a little frightened by the intensity of her feelings.

From then on, she treated her bewildered mother with absolute scorn. Like a cockroach, to be trodden on. She became bored and more and more greedy, lolling around with the boys in the band, down at the park or at the dance hall, determined to find a way to leave her stupid mother to her just deserts. Planning and waiting.

*

Down in the Bistro Bar at the bottom end of the alpine village, the locals were enjoying their Saturday dance to the somewhat dubious beat of the Brown Ones. Bettina's appearance hardly altered their tempo, excepting possibly the guy on the sax, who may have missed a beat. Her fantastic garb never raised an eyebrow in the jeans brotherhood that writhed and gyrated across the floor.

Only one unlovely kid uttered a low 'Christ! What a size,' as she elbowed her way to the bar.

'A coupla beers, Chris.'

'How yer been, Bett?' She shrugged and carried the two beers to a table in the corner. She sat and smoked but didn't touch a glass.

When the band stopped for a break, the guy on the sax flopped into the chair beside her, legs stretched across the floor and drained the glass in front of him. Finally, 'How's the kid?'

'What's it to you?'

'She's my kid, ain't she?'

'For all you care. I need some money. She's gotta get her teeth fixed'

'Aw, yeah?'

'Yeah.'

'Well, I ain't got none. I'm short, see. And what about that baboon upstairs? Don't he pay yer?'

'I've gotta live, yer know.'

'Yeah, on the grog. 'Ere, 'ave yer beer.'

'No thanks.' She lit a cigarette. 'Please, Andy,' she suddenly pleaded, 'I need forty dollars.'

'Aw, Christ!' He angrily lurched to his feet and feeling in his back pocket produced a tattered wallet. 'Money, money, money, that's all you ever think of.' He drew out a twenty-dollar bill and threw it on the table. 'That's it – all I got, believe it or not.'

She crumpled the note in her hand. 'Where'll you be next week?'

'As if I'd tell yer,' he sneered. 'And if you don't quit followin' me around, one day I might just ring yer bloody neck. That is, if I could git me 'ands around it.' He laughed uproariously. 'That's good,' he said. 'What a joke.' And still amused with himself, he slouched off towards the bar.

She ground the cigarette beneath her heel. 'Oh God,' she said breathlessly, 'I might as well…'

They waited through the following evening in the overcrowded upstairs restaurant all eager with anticipation, but she did not come. When the smell of goulash had finally settled and the red wine carafes were empty, when it was finally so late, Bruno, with an apologetic shrug, was forced to admit, 'Ladies and gentlemen, I am so sorry but she must haff gone.'

*

No one ever saw her again, though apparently a guy playing the sax was doing the rounds dragging a kid along – his shiralee. A young girl. BB he called her.

Hitchhikers

Lately I've thrown caution to the wind and begun picking up hitchhikers. Why not, I ask – we live in a small community where buses, trains, trams are rare or non-existent. Not too many people would waste time standing and raising a hand if they had a better choice.

George was amazed that I'd stopped for him, 'You're taking a risk picking up a bloke like me,' he admonished.

But George and I found we had a lot in common, including the mechanic we both used and where he was headed to collect his car. By the time I dropped him off, we were on a first-name basis and hoped to meet en route another day.

And then there was Kirsty – late for school *again* after a row with her mum because she hadn't fed the dog. 'You wanted this dog and you promised you'd look after him but it's always me that does everything,' her mother had stormed as she readied herself for work, 'and don't think I'm driving you to school again, because I'm not. And if you'd get your face out of that bloody phone and go to bed at a reasonable hour, you wouldn't sleep in.'

I gave her a tissue and sympathised. Tears were dried, nose noisily blown and we managed the drop-off just in time to save further distress to an already very stressed teenager.

She gave me a droopy smile. 'Wish you were me mum,' she waved, slinging her pack over her shoulder.

Yesterday I met Bob. He wasn't exactly hitching but he was standing trying to catch his breath halfway up the hill to the store.

He gladly hobbled over as I held the door. 'Aw thanks, luv,' he said. 'Didn't realise me hip was so bad – that bloomin hill's a bugger.' He patted my leg. 'Yer an angel.' he said with a sigh of relief. Bob lived alone and was store-bound in need of milk for his morning cuppa. 'You'd think I could do without me milk,' he said, with such a twinkle in his eye, 'but it just don't taste the same.'

Of course I drove him home again and as I pulled up at the front gate he leaned over so appealingly, saying, 'Yer'll come and share it with me, won't yer, luv?'

I couldn't resist. I looked at my watch. Sure, the rest can wait. And he made my day, this dear old man, he really made my day.

The tiny wooden cottage must have been built in the timber heydays, but it was as neat as a new pin (wherever that old saying comes from), cosy, warm and inviting. And the old iron kettle simmered on the probably even older fuel stove just waiting for Bob to fill the teapot. Which he did covering it with a chirpy, striped, knitted tea cosy while we waited for it to draw.

My admiration for his housekeeping was answered with 'I'd be denying Ellen if I didn't keep up standards.'

Ellen, his dearly beloved wife of sixty-one years, had only recently died but Bob was determined not to let her down. 'I promised,' he said, 'just before she went, I'd look after meself and that I will.' He rustled in a drawer for some serviettes as he served the biscuits with our milky tea, and cut my 'Don't fuss' with 'Ellen would'a give yer one.'

A deep red rose stood in the little vase on the table, its perfume adding to a slow feeling of contentment that began to seep through me.

'Ellen loved 'er roses,' Bob observed.

I wished time would stop. I wanted to melt into this old man's days, embraced within his genuine simplicity and love. But with a sigh I roused myself from his world, heading back into something rather bleak and meaningless.

'See ya, Bob,' I said,. 'Thanks for the cuppa, and look after that hip.'

'Come in any time, luv,' he smiled as he began to clear the table.

Hitchhikers – well, maybe they're not a bad lot.

I Do Love Trains

I do love trains, she thought as she gently subsided into the window seat looking forward to the many hours ahead – nothing to disturb her peace, blessed time to think, relax, read and take in the view.

She sipped takeaway station latte – its mediocre quality was not enough to reduce her expectations – warming her hands, leaning comfortably back as she contemplated whether to start on the crossword or her new book.

The loud startling thump as somebody flopped roughly into the seat behind caused her to sit up, the mouthful going down the wrong way and in her spluttering spilling coffee on her decent jeans. Mid-cough, she turned to face a swarthy teenager who just at that moment kicked the footrest into submission and slammed down the food tray with the force of a boxer in training.

Too shocked and startled, she could only glare. He stuck his head into a grubby supermarket bag and hauled out some earphones. Wiping up, she resettled, gingerly, searching for her equilibrium in the hope of restoring law and order into her small space. A space that had become considerably less in the last few minutes.

'Jeez, mate – 'ow are yer? Saw yez gettin' on from the other carriage. Watcha doin' 'ere? Out on remand?' A replica kid chucked down his pack and flung himself into the other seat.

She held fast to her fragile cup prepared for…what, she hated to think.

'Yer OK?' the newcomer asked.

'Yeah. Out fer a few days before I go to court.'

'Where yer 'eadin'?'

'Mum's. She met me bail.'

'Jeez,' he kicked the back of the seat, 'then what? Will them fuck-wits send yer back?'

''Spose.'

'Wanna go back?'

'Reckon. Best food. 'Cept for breakfast. Git yer up at six every morning just ter eat.'

'What other juvies been with yer – not those arse'oles…?'

'Na not them. I was pretty safe. Not like that other fuckin' shit'ole – raped us the moment we was chucked in. Be on me bike before I'd let them send me back there.'

What is happening? She held her forehead in disbelief. This was worse than the worst of movies. She sat frozen. Juvenile offenders. Sitting in *her* train. Wrecking *her* day and not in any way caring, yelling out for all to hear, laughing and swearing and thumbing their noses. She was so agitated she didn't know what to do. Her eyes searched for the conductor but she wasn't game to move. Opened her book. Pretended to read. The words floated by unseen as her mind grabbed at those other words roughly tossed around behind her, orchestrated by raucous laughter and then – a hard punch.

'Hey, quit it. Yer worse than that fuckin' islander in me cell – they 'ad ter git the riot team in. Yeah and the sniffer dog too – lookin' fer white sugar. Some of the boys stuck shit up its nose. Jeez, I cracked up. Yeah, just like I laughed when I beat up that filthy Moslem. Broke 'is face. 'it 'im like 'ell. I 'it 'im an' 'e fell an' I stamped on 'im.'

She could feel his blood rising, his excitement as he slapped his legs and was horrified.

'Poor stupid bugger tried ter git up an' I jumped on 'im again an' blood came outa 'is ear.'

She was trembling but realised now it was more from anger than fear. Anger at the violence; at his pride in it. She didn't know the legacy these kids grew up with. They learnt early from a brother, an uncle, a neighbour – feral farmers they called themselves. In the business, so to speak. She felt filled like a huge balloon ready to burst. Breathe deeply, she instructed herself as she tried looking at the countryside – peaceful and green after so much rain. Cows munched with not a care in the world. She envied them their composure.

'Yeah, well, serve the bugger right. All the same these fuckin' terrorists – shoulda finished 'im off.'

'…and they can't use force on us juveniles, though they're so full of shit I wouldn't trust the weasels.'

She was angry to have been exposed to such behaviour. She'd lived with stockmen and shearers, tough, hard men who'd always held their tongues in front of women. Now she was furious to be so impotent: so lacking in knowledge and so intimidated. She hated them with a missionary's venom.

Intent on her outrage, it was a few minutes before she sensed a change. She struggled now to hear them.

'…yeah, me dad ain't never been around much. I seen 'im sometimes – seemed to come just ter beat up Mum, the bastard,' he said softly, longingly, 'but I'd talk ter 'im if I saw 'im in the street.'

'Better 'n me. Never 'ad a dad. Dunno 'ow I'm 'ere. Must be magic.' He laughed apologetically, but added, 'Me ole' lady went off with some bugger. 'e 'ated me like I was rat shit. But where'll they send yer, do yer reckon. Yer know…after?'

'Dunno but anywhere away from those fuckin' rapists. It'll be OK if I get to go to school. Give me a bit of time out from whatever piss joint they chuck me in.'

They lapsed into a calmer silence at last, and she wondered what thoughts were loud in their heads.

Slowly, strangely she felt her body slacken with a long slow release of breath. The air seemed to ease out of her as if the balloon had been punctured and now lay deflated and wrinkled on the ground. Tension and anger had evaporated and in its place a new, raw emotion took hold, a dawning understanding that rolled in and filled her with an extraordinary and inexplicable need. She suddenly wanted to take these two, lost, lonely and misunderstood 'babies' into her arms and give them love. They'd have laughed if they'd known, scoffed at her pity.

Quietly, they were planning their escapade for the night now that darkness had descended and they were nearly there. 'Neat little break and entry. Yeah. Grab a car and head off.' Not in their town of course. It had been drummed into them, that wasn't done; they had their principles and this was their way of life.

No chance things would ever change. No way they wanted it to.

Soup

I've always detested tomato soup.

'How could you?' my husband would say. 'There's just nothing to dislike about tomato soup. Especially if you buy the Aussie extra ruby red brand.'

Well, I know I've told him the reason but he simply chooses to forget, especially when we're in the supermarket and we pass the shelves filled with can after can and brand after brand of mouth-watering (to him) tomato soup.

'Little Brownie,' my grandmother had called down the long echoing veranda when I was about eight, 'I think I'll make soup and use up some of those tomatoes in the vegetable garden. Be a sweet child and run down and fill this basket for me.'

I was not an enthusiastic helper in those days and crossly grabbed the basket as I headed towards the stairs.

'But put on your shoes, darling. You never know what you might step on.'

'I'm all right,' I grumpily replied, and down I went through the cellar, across the chook yard, past the well, the terrifying turkeys and over to the picket gate.

The vegie garden was my green-fingered grandfather's pride and joy. The food he produced was miraculous and the tomatoes this year seemed to beam with pride saying, 'Eat me, I am beautiful.' Even I, who stubbornly refused salads, would often sneak over and pick a couple. It was like feasting on a juicy apple except that the stains on my face and clothes left no doubt as to what I'd been up to. 'Down in Grandad's patch again, eh?' someone was sure to say.

My legs trudged across to the other side of the garden but my mind had me halfway up to the stables to groom and cuddle my pony, so that as I stretched out a hand to grab the first huge tomato, I was unaware of where I trod. Suddenly a terrible stinging sensation tore up my foot and leg. I screamed, dropped the basket, sat rubbing, felt more stings in the other leg and my hands, completely unable to comprehend what was happening until, looking down, I realised I was in the middle of a clump of stinging nettles.

Now, I don't know if you have ever experienced the pain of these nettles – I had not (and hope never to again) but my poor skinny body seemed to be burning alive. I called and cried, tears streaming down my cheeks, I called and ran and called again but nobody heard; the house was up the hill some hundreds of yards away. I felt utterly abandoned. How could they send me on such a terrible journey, to let me get stung, those strong-grown ups and I'm just little me. It's not fair, I cried, trying to run and rub, stumbling blindly towards help, my sobbing louder than the flapping turkey gobblers.

The screams had, in fact, attracted attention and there were loving and sympathetic arms at the top of the steps.

'Poor wee thing. Quick, grab the cold cloth, pass the ammonia. There, there, sweetheart. We'll get you into a cool bath. You'll soon feel better.'

They hugged and soothed and dried my eyes.

'Ah well,' said Gran, sturdily stoking the fuel stove, 'I did tell her to put on shoes.'

Man's Best Friend

He hadn't wanted to make this visit, felt dreadful about it, but truth to tell, he just couldn't understand his daughter. Never had. And the older he got and the older she got, the worse it had become. Never having married probably made it more difficult and the word spinster really seemed to describe her well. She was skinny and crabby and bossy and generally no fun to be around.

'She's had an unhappy time of it, Mike,' his wife Alice used to say. 'Life just hasn't gone her way.'

'Yeah, well, she hasn't helped life much either,' he'd replied, leaving her to be peacemaker.

Now, six months after his wife's sudden death, he had taken the plunge, for Alice's sake, he told the others in the Village, and hopped on the train north. It was stressful from the moment he got there. The timetable had been changed and his arrival meant Melissa must leave work early to collect him. He was in big trouble for not having warned her and collapsed with a sigh on the hard modern sofa already regretful he'd made this rather hasty decision. Especially when Melissa's recent acquisition, a smelly small dog of unknown origins, insisted on moulting all over his good trousers.

Nearly losing his neck, as there was no comfortable headrest like their old chair back home, he let out a gasp. His eyes had focused on the mantelpiece. Agog with horror and consternation, there was no way he could stop the words from coming out of his mouth. 'My God! What the hell's going on? What on earth are all those urns?'

His daughter dashed in, anxious. 'What's the matter, Dad?' she frowned, the frozen chicken legs and the broccoli (oh, not more broccoli, he had time to think – she feeds me nothing but broccoli) still in her hands. 'I've got to get these defrosted or we'll never eat.'

'Those b-b-bloody urns,' he pointed, stuttering in dismay. 'What are they doing there?'

'What do you think they're doing?' she flared resentfully and then tearfully, 'They're my darlings Pogo and Ming and of course,' she lowered her voice and her eyes respectfully, 'the green one is some of Mum's ashes. What's wrong with that? They're all I've got,' she nearly whined and then brightened, 'Except now I've got little Tuffy.' She crossed to the sofa and ruffled the mutt's neck. 'He keeps me warm at night.'

Mike had forgotten the two deaths in the last year or so and felt slightly awkward but still the garish display was too much and putting them on a par with his beloved wife – God, what's the woman thinking? And is she bloody sleeping with the dog?

'Waddya mean, he keeps you warm at night?'

'What do you think I mean? He snuggles in beside me, don't you, my little man?' she cooed, stroking him again. 'Right against my heart.'

It was too much for Mike. He heaved the dog onto the floor and struggled off the sofa. 'I gotta get some fresh air.'

'Good idea,' she replied, 'and while you're out there, you might look at the hose fitting. I just can't get it to stay on. And the window lock seems jammed too and can you…'

He blocked his ears. Here it comes, always the same whenever we came to stay: I spent my time being Mr Fixit. Well, I've had enough of it. I'm too old for this caper.

However, he did fix most of her problems, kept him out of the house and away from the urns, but after a couple of days he could take it no more and made the excuse of a forgotten long-awaited doctor's appointment to return home. He boarded the train with some sadness but great relief.

Being home wasn't good either, though it was better than it had been since Alice's death. For months, he'd not moved from the darkened sitting room where he watched TV inanely, never remembering what he'd seen. He made some attempt to keep the house clean but rarely got out of his pyjamas, hardly ate, spoke to few. Those kind neighbours who tried to brighten his days gave up in the end. Those who offered tempting dishes were turned away too often. Even the minister found more responsive people to counsel.

A week or so after he got back, he was, as usual, watching something mindless on the telly when the doorbell rang – long and insistently. It frightened him out of his wits – nobody ever seemed to ring his doorbell these days. 'Who the devil...' he muttered, nearly taking a tumble as he struggled up from the chair. 'Hang on, hang on ...' he grumbled as he fiddled with the lock – and there she was.

Bessie, from a couple of doors down and in a terrible state, weeping. Mike hadn't seen her for a while, knew her husband had died some time ago, but not much else.

He stepped out as the fly screen slammed shut, and held her by the shoulders. 'Hey, hey there, Bessie, what's up? Come, come, calm down. It'll be all right. Tell me what's the problem.'

Then it happened. She fell against him resting her head on his chest, warm and comforting for her throbbing body. And for a moment they stood, both registering something – but what? They weren't quite sure. A kind of relief. Mike realised then just what it was he'd been longing for but Bessie bringing out a saturated hankie broke the moment and they stepped back silently embarrassed.

'Oh, I'm sorry to bother you, Mike, but I couldn't find anyone to help – Sheila and Don next door are away and Madge on the other side goes to church and the office is closed and I don't mean to bother you but...' she rattled on like a rushing train and tears began to flow again, a waterfall of frustration and loneliness, 'but I just can't turn the tap off and Jim always did these things and I don't...'

'Shush,' he patted her hand. 'Come on, let's go...probably only needs a new washer.' Mike was all action – he was needed.

And that was the beginning. How deeply profound it was to feel alive again. To once more savour the softness of touch, the simplicity of sharing a cuppa and the pleasure of telling a yarn. Now when the sun shone on a new day, Mike was beaming too and he jumped out of bed with purpose, his mind filled with things they would do.

After Jim died, Bessie had hung about with a couple of other women in the village. The were known as the Gossiping Girls but Bessie didn't care; it was somebody to talk to. Jim had reckoned the two big ones were like a couple of Rottweilers but the smaller one was more furry – a fox terrier, he called her. Well, the Rottweilers were not at all impressed with the romance. 'Just jealous, they know a good-looking guy when they see one,' joked Jim, more than joyful with his sprightly little Foxy.

While there were plenty who were pleased to witness this happy scenario – among them were Bessie's daughters, who were glad their flighty mum had someone to look after her and reckoned Mike was a good old bloke – there were others not so enthusiastic.

Some of the sourpusses in the Village would pass remarks: 'Really, at their age, moving in together – you've got to be joking.'

'He'll soon get sick of taking her dancing.'

'She'll have to put up with his terrible snoring,' and so on.

But Melissa's barbs were the worst. She was furious. 'Really, Dad, you must be out of your mind getting the hots for some floozy you hardly know. What's got into you?' she fumed over the phone. When he tried to explain, she'd have none of it. 'Loneliness? What rot, you don't know anything about loneliness, and I'm not having some little bit sneaking in and taking what deserves to be mine. I can just see it – she'll wait till you kark it and then she'll be laughing. Just don't be a stupid old fool.'

'It's not like that, Melissa, we…'

His words were drowned out by her yelling. 'Dad,' the fire in her voice could have melted the lines, 'I'm coming to get you. I want you to come and live with Tuffy and me. Right now.'

'What'll I do about her?' Mike pondered over coffee with Bessie.

'Bit of a hide, I'd say,' she replied. 'After all, it's OK for her to go to bed with a stinking dog but not for you to hop between the sheets with a gorgeous gal.' She smiled and leant over to kiss him.

'I know…' He burst out laughing. 'We'll get married termorrer. That'll fix her.'

My Favourite Shoes 1

It was painful to be so tall as a young teenager and embarrassing when the boys only came up to my chin. Dancing class was the worst. That agonising wait to see if I'd be chosen to dance the quickstep and avoid the humiliation of being a wallflower. I was no beauty either, so I felt badly handicapped on those suburban Thursday nights. Of course I wore flatter than flat shoes hoping that some boy could possibly look me in the eye. I would be grateful for any of the species to take my hand no matter how dumb or pimply.

Since then, even to this day, I've longed for a pair of superbly high, sexy, designer shoes. All my life I envied those girls who tripped about in luscious footwear while I scuffed along in my old flatties. Work, marriage, kids: there never seemed to be the money, or a reason, to treat my feet to some elegance.

Occasionally while buying school wear for the kids, or a shirt for hubby, I'd pause wistfully outside a shoe shop, but, busy en route to take somebody someplace in a hurry, it was never more than a hopeless glimpse.

Life wandered on in my usual flat-footed way until I won a trip to Paris. Online! Apparently I clicked on something trying to navigate round a screen full of ads looking for info on Sartre, when Hurrah! Flashing lights and jumping stars! You've won! My muddled mind could hardly take it in.

To cut a long story short, six months later I was flying into Le Bourget, my body a tingle at the prospect of spending a week in the most romantic city in the world. My excitement was not at the thought of seeing the famous city sights, soaking up the history, browsing through the museums, laying eyes on an original Monet, Cezanne or Renoir.

No, I was off in a different direction. I was off to see other galleries. Other works of art. Gallery Lafayette and Printemps, searching for the ultimate in perfection – a pair of designer shoes.

I was breathless with joy and anticipation. Every day and half the nights, I roamed the city – down the Champs Elysées, Boulevarde St Germain, Rue de Bonaparte, Rue de Rivoli, thrilled to the bone with the glorious sight of shoes, shoes, shoes. Such glamour, such style, such sophistication, a never-ending delight. I hardly ate. I hardly slept.

And then suddenly, the day before I was due to fly out, it happened. Love at first sight. There they were. Excruciatingly high, shockingly pink, patient leather, diamond-studded and bowed. 'Exquisite' by Christian Louboutin.

My flight home was at fever pitch. The gold-wrapped package clutched close, never out of my sight. I couldn't wait to parade my *raison d'être*, my favourite ever pair of shoes. I posed for the family, model like, sauntering slinkily down the concrete path.

I've no idea what happened. One moment I was upright, the next writhing on the ground in searing pain. Too shocked I hardly heard their voices.

'Is it broken?'

'My God, look how it's twisted.'

'Quick, get those dreadful shoes off.'

'Ring the doctor.'

'Yes,' he said, 'nasty one. Always takes time for these multiple fractures to mend. She'll need some flat supportive shoes of course, with the crutches and the walker. Four-inch heels,' he was heard to mumble, 'at her age…must be off her rocker.'

My Favourite Shoes 2

My name is Indy. I am five and today I am wearing my favourite pair of shoes. They are my new soccer boots and they are bright sparkly pink with beautiful silver laces. They match my pink beanie and my pink and white striped socks that my team wears.

We are called the Pittwater Princesses and we also wear red shorts and long red shirts. My shirt has my name on it and my number. I am number 1 but Auntie Min says she cannot tell as my ponytail hangs down over it. I don't know why we have numbers. My friend Lola is number 6.

My shoes make my feet dance and I do a lot of skipping on the soccer field. And little jumps. Sometimes I get near the ball and sometimes I kick it. Often I don't know where the ball is because I like watching the birds in the trees and scrunching up my fingers in my new pink striped gloves when it's very cold.

Auntie Min calls, 'Go, Indy, kick it.'

I ran so fast I missed it but Auntie Min clapped and called 'Good try' anyway. Then after half-time we couldn't find the ball. We didn't know where it was and Mr Mackie, our coach (he's nice, he's Georgia's dad) was calling everywhere, 'Where's my ball?' Then we saw Sam, he's playing for the Duffers against us, just sitting on it. They wear black and white striped shirts and don't look nearly as pretty as we do.

Crystal didn't want to play any more, so Gemma came on instead and we held hands and went running together. I like Gemma but Crystal always goes crying to her mother. My dad comes to soccer with me.

I think the boys won but we all had jelly snakes afterwards. Mine was red – my favourite. It matches my shirt. My boots got a bit dirty and Auntie Min helped me to clean them with a tissue, so I am going to show her my chickens, especially Michael Clarke, who is a bit sick. They are Silkies.

We all went and shook hands and Lola got an award. Mr Mackie said it was because she had touched the ball five times when last week she hadn't touched it once. Maybe I'll get a certificate next week. Right now, Auntie Min wants me to change out of my boots but I don't want to. They are my very favourite pair of shoes.

One Day in My Life, by Bertrand Ostrich

I hate it when she brings all the family over to inspect us – like we're some kind of curiosity.

'Don't put your fingers through the wire,' she instructs the squawky kid. 'Their beaks can really nip you. Might even swallow ring man for dinner,' she teases.

Well, maybe that would be fair enough since she keeps getting in and taking our eggs. She did it again yesterday. Captured Blanche's latest, perfect, glowing beauty. I'd been sitting on it, keeping the temperature just right, until she called us up the other end of the run. She had some crispy fresh spinach to go with our evening nibbles. Blanche got to it first and while we were having a little argument about my share, that rotten Milly crept through the bottom gate and snitched the egg.

Poor Blanche was in tears. 'Not again!' she cried, stamping and flapping her wings. Now she's blaming me for leaving my post and is huffing up her feathers in the top corner.

Milly's just so sneaky she always finds a way to get our eggs. We spend ages searching for a place to lay where she can't see them but she's so hard to trick. She made us a nest with fresh hay the other day but we're not stupid, we know what she's up to putting it near the fence, where she can drag out the egg with a rake and not have to come into the yard. Of course she knows how crabby we can get and, as I heard her tell young Brian from next door, 'dangerous', when we're upset or frightened. I could tear her side open, if I felt like it, with one great downward slash of my leg. We don't have long hard nails for nothing and they can rip open anything quicker than an axe.

But we like Milly pretty well. She's always coming to chat and rub our necks through the fence. She experiments with different feed but we're a fussy lot. I like rolled barley but Blanche only wants the pellets.

We've lived here since we were four months old and it's a nice place. Now we're laying our first eggs and watch the younger ostriches in the other yards as they rush around flapping their feathers and hooting – acting like a lot of crazy kids. The other day, they nearly went ballistic when the helicopter flew over inspecting the power lines – I thought they'd break a leg rushing into the fences. We did that a bit before we got used to the noise; now it doesn't bother us so much.

It's school holidays at the moment and she's got her grandchildren staying. They come and put the feed in our bins after she's shut the shed door on our side. The door isn't in good shape since I backed into it when the vet came to give me an injection. I can't stand the black hood they put over our heads but he got it on before I could manage a kick and I just couldn't move an inch. It's too dark. I get confused.

The kids clean up a bit (think she pays them some holiday money) and give us our shell grit. It tasted a bit salty the other day, so reckon they'd collected it from the beach. Makes strong eggs, they say. I don't know about that. We cracked one last week when it landed on a stone. Milly went wild – she'd lose dollars and I mean *dollars*. We got no spinach that night.

It's been terribly hot lately and that squawky kid waters us with the hose. Blanche loves it down her neck and particularly the fine spray on her face. The kid's good at that, I must say, and his little sister dances round like a fairy, giggling.

'Do it again,' she laughs. 'I want to see her wriggling her bum feathers. She looks so cute.'

Yeah, well, I can wriggle mine better, so I give a hoot and barge in to get a cool off too.

'Come on, kids,' calls Milly. 'You can do them again later. Just fill their water and turn off the tap. Watch out for that Bertrand, though, he's pretty stroppy at the moment. Just look at his legs, they're red as red.'

'So how did they get red, Granny?' asks the fairy girl. 'They weren't like that yesterday.'

'He's ready to mate, sweetheart,' says Milly.

'What's that mean?'

'Let's get off to the beach,' comes the reply. 'I'll explain on the way.'

Well, maybe she will and maybe she won't, but Blanche and I will have a little peace and quiet for a bit. We'll just sit together in the corner and watch those stupid cows munching mindlessly in the other paddock.

Broken Hearts

He stole our hearts – all our hearts – just lobbing in onto the patio table.

It was unbelievable at first. I particularly was amazed that a small bird would begin a conversation with me as if we were lifelong friends. It was Sunday morning. Our day of rest. My day of slippers and no make-up. We'd finished toast and were just up to coffee, deliriously relaxed in the summer sun, when he arrived.

Quite spellbound, even the two boisterous boys, we froze, watching this petite person neatly picking his way up my arm, then across my shoulder and finally to my neck which he began to nibble. I couldn't help a giggle at the tickle and he seemed to regard that as a sign for more. When I curled my hand around the tiny body to extricate him from my hair, he didn't struggle, just blinked at me as if it was all perfectly normal and acceptable.

Slowly our voices returned and we whispered at the wonder of it, taking turns to stroke and cuddle. Soon concern filtered in with the sunlight. Where does he belong? What should we do? How to keep him safe?

So the boys rushed next door, sure the neighbours had an old cage. I followed with him on my shoulder but just inside he suddenly took off. Imagine my terror as he flew towards their little black kitten. It happened too quickly for anyone to move and by the time we did, there was no need, as the two became instant friends. We watched entranced as they played. He pecked and poked; she cuffed and danced. It was a magic like no other. A delight to see that joy can be shared any time between the most unlikely of strangers.

It was decided we would keep him in the cage while searching for his owners but as the boys climbed over the fence, a dog barked. This previously calm and fearless little creature instantly became a ferocious beast, screeching and flapping wildly, determined to escape. And escape he did. Somehow he squeezed his terrified tiny body through the bars, and in a flash of red and green had disappeared into the trees.

We searched and called until well after dark, left food in convenient places, but morning brought no signs of his whereabouts. We dared not speak of the cruelty of the bush or the impossibility of his survival amongst the wild birds; those thoughts were too painful. Sundays for a long while were our sad days and even now, half a lifetime later, we'll softly muse about a little green bird who not only stole our hearts, but broke them too.

The Clowns: A Modern-day Fable

Once upon a time, there was a woman who left her home and friends to make a long journey to a southern land. She carried her special possessions, as she was leaving forever to live with the man she cared about more than any other.

This was a difficult decision for the woman, considering all that had not passed between them over some years. All the words not spoken, the thoughts not shared, the emotions hidden; but she longed to be with him in joy and peace.

As she began the journey, her whole being was filled with excitement and anticipation. He was probably excited too after long years alone but felt wary and wondering. So many expectations for them both.

Sadly, expectations were not realisations. Too soon, the oasis dried up. Disillusionment was a sad state to be in but she stayed on, trying to belong in this new place, hoping time would bind them, longing for the kind of love she'd hoped they would give each other.

Once, after an argument, she purchased two small, enchanting (to her mind) glass clowns. A peace offering. One for him and one for her. An ode to joy for them to share. That night, she softly gave him one of them. But his reaction was hurtful and dismissive, so she never told him there were two. Only a few days later, she found the smiling little fellow broken on the floor. The man's indifference stung, yet she glued it together and replaced it; but the crack showed – the imperfection left her with an innate sadness.

There followed an aimless time, since the big goal, the ultimate reason for her being there, seemed to have eluded them. Eventually she returned to her hometown, taking back all her precious possessions as well as the little clown. Strangely, he followed and when she placed both clowns (his and hers) together on the shelf, he chose not to notice. Despite their prominent position, it was as if, to him, they didn't exist. Like their love? He never once mentioned them in those tedious years before he drifted away back to his own land.

Alone, not long after the man had gone, the woman found a sad array of broken glass; coloured shapes lying helpless on the shelf. Shattered pieces of fun and joy. No longer clowns. No longer anything.

She shivered suddenly at last understanding that the little clowns were a symbol of their relationship. Broken. Absolutely beyond repair.

My Day of Enlightenment

The Golden Days Retirement Resort certainly lived up to expectations. It was all those glossy ads said and maybe even more. I was thrilled to bits.

'You'll love it, Mum,' all the kids insisted, joining forces in their push to get me to sell the house and start anew after Dad died. I must admit, I found it very hard when he finally went. There had been years of caring for the poor old darling once Alzheimer's was diagnosed.

Trying to keep him busy as he followed me round like a big puppy was a full-time job and later on, when dressing him was impossible and he became incontinent, well, it really did become too much. I agonised – we all did, mind you – about putting him in a home, but we found a beautiful place overlooking the ocean where he could pace about and they were such angels there. They became part of my family they were just so good to Dad. That one blessing I am glad of. But then it was all so quiet. I wasn't needed any more, so I didn't resist the idea of a change of scenery too much.

'But how will I ever get out of this house?' I asked. A lifetime of junk and treasures to be sorted and sent to Vinnies. I couldn't bear the thought.

'Just don't you worry yourself about that, Mum,' they said. 'We'll work it all out.'

One thing I am lucky about. Even if I do say so, I have wonderful children.

So here I am. Living a life of luxury I would never have dreamt of. Dad and I weren't into all that kind of stuff – camping and picnics and the odd stay in a cabin is what we did. Never wanted more.

It took a while to settle in. I'm a bit shy really. But everybody was so nice and when Miriam suggested a party I was all for it. I was getting used to having a few little tipples before dinner at night – Dad and I rarely drank alcohol, except when the children got married, and even then it was a bit of pretend. But I must say I'm really quite fond of the red wine we've been having lately.

I kind of dressed up a bit the night of the party. It was really good fun. You should have seen all the food they turned on. And champagne. I seem to have quite a taste for that too. It does do funny things to you, though, doesn't it?

Suddenly this old boy was sitting on my lap saying, 'Come on now, Lizzie, give us a peck.'

Everyone was giggling and so was I. Wow, what a pasho kisser, and do you know what? I rather liked it. The rest of the night we behaved like, oh, I guess a bit like lovesick teenagers do.

Next morning, Shirley from the room next door asked how I was.

'Great,' I said. 'Why?'

'Oh,' she replied, 'I thought you might be feeling a bit embarrassed the way you went on with old Dave last night.'

Well, I'm blowed if I know why she said that. I feel as if I'm suddenly starting to live.

In fact, I think yesterday was my day of enlightenment.

The Last Laugh

It's interesting to wonder what glues couples together. Some appear perfectly in tune, so the question doesn't arise, but others seem totally out of sync, and there's the mystery. If you were a fly on the wall at Matt and Meryl's, I'm sure you'd end up buzzing around in circles quite confused by the incessant, seemingly pointless, futile feuding that looks like their *raison d'être*. Domestic violence, you might say, with a capital V, though not a hand is laid on one or the other, no physical contact ever exchanged. Their war of words is more potent and more poisonous than any bodily confrontation – a slow venomous infiltration of malice blocking any road to peace and harmony.

You'd flutter your wings in frustration at their mindless squabbling. There wouldn't be a conversation that didn't become a heated argument – whether on the subject of what to have for dinner or how many blankets to pull up at night or which TV program to watch. An argument that almost always ended with a final, under his breath but perfectly loud enough to hear, 'I didn't start this.' Matt was determined to have the last word.

'You always have to make it into an argument,' he would say, adamant that it was never ever his fault. His sanctimonious attitude was unbelievable.

Sometimes Meryl let it get the better of her and shouted back, other times she imagined she was bubbling like her mother's pea soup when it frothed over the side of the saucepan and crawled across the stove. No wonder sleep crept under her bed and left her tossing on a rough sea of curling sheets. To a fly on the wall, the thought came that a soft touch, a gentle kiss on the neck or even an apology might have worked wonders on those nights.

And looking back, that is how it had been in the early days – they rather enjoyed their banter. Sometimes it started as teasing and she could manage that. At first anyway. Latterly when he would criticise her and she reacted, he would come up with 'Just teasing – can't you take a joke.' Of course she couldn't, because it wasn't funny any more. Once, when all might have been remedied in the bedroom, it was OK but these days they didn't even share a room let alone a bed.

The most persistent issue was Matt's addiction. Newspapers. His daily routine was based on the perusal, over and over, of the *Herald*, the local rag, the *New Scientist*, *The National Geographic*, the *Community Chronicle*, the *Northern News*, or *The Seniors Travel Journal*. Bits were torn from here and underlined there, cut-out piles were dumped untidily on the small round table (always getting in the way of Meryl's African violet) and the 'to be read again' pages were shoved under his chair (his chair, mind you; nobody else was expected to sit there).

Meryl, years ago, had fixed up an old paper rack she'd bought at the op shop to try and encourage some order, but it remained annoyingly empty. 'Really,' she'd complain, 'why can't you at least put the magazines in that rack? What do you think I got it for?'

'Well, I didn't ask you to get it, did I?' he demanded belligerently. 'Why do you have to go on and on about everything? Who cares if there's a bit of a mess around the place? You are just so pedantic.'

Pedantic was a word he loved to employ, and it annoyed Meryl intensely, particularly as he applied it in an incorrect non-academic way. He persistently offered it up to friends he might corner at one get together or another as he let it be known what a perfectionist his wife had become. Of course the word was used in a derogatory way, intimating that being tidy was not a quality of merit. Slyly he would lower his eyes, studying his rather effeminate fingers with a quiet sigh, hoping to create sympathy for his difficult position.

He was a good actor, Meryl had to admit. Never let a chance go by when he could, in the nicest possible 'I'm such a good guy' way, clarify his truly downtrodden position in the household. If you hadn't met Meryl, didn't know her well, you would be forgiven for thinking she was a real bitch. Her friends, however, were au fait with these domestic tribulations, understood the absolute power Matt wielded, and wondered why she stayed. And that takes me back to my first point of interest.

Why do such couples stay together? Some kind of comfort zone? But what comfort is such discomfort? And getting back to the newspapers – just a part actually of Matt's disruption of the living room – makes one aware (as a fly on the wall) of Meryl's problem. Matt does little these days except loll in his chair doing the crossword when he has finished the papers, eating and sleeping through the day while she is being pedantic cleaning up after him. First there's the peanut butter from lunch curling on the carpet under a hailstorm of bread crumbs, and then there's the old sandals plopped off on the white mat dropping dried mud from the driveway.

'Just sit down and relax,' he'd say. 'You never stop.'

'Well, who will clean up if I don't?' she retorts. 'And just look at this filthy chair – even the arm covers are beyond cleaning.'

'Oh dear, dear, is there a tiny itty bitty dirt on the arm? Oh goodness, quick, quick let me scrub it off – someone might come and see it.' He'd pretend to industriously rub with his shirt, behaving like a two-year-old. Except a two-year-old would be sent to his room to do time out for being so rude.

If a fly happened to be nearby, Matt could be heard on the phone whingeing about his lot. 'Meryl? Yes, she's OK. Never stops. Always complaining of the mess I make of the basin or the toilet or something. She's such a pedant. Yes, you're right, bloody hard to live with.'

Matt was a mean-spirited man in actual fact. An only child, he was self-indulged and thoroughly spoiled by his doting mother, which led him to believe that his comfort was number one priority and all that really mattered.

Three wives had left him, seven children scattered around the continent, so that must lead you to question his credentials. Of course it was always the wives' fault (nasty pieces, the lot of them) that the relationships didn't work. And the kids? Well…they just took after their mothers; what would you expect? Forget the little bastards – he had better things to do. And better things, apparently, was to make life as unpleasant as possible for Meryl. He sincerely felt he was hard done by. Why should a man at his time of life have to fuss over cleaning the saucepans and putting out the compost before the maggots got in? He deserved better and felt quite justified in making plans to ensure Meryl would get, as he called it, her just deserts.

He knew the usual tricks – the ones that raised her ire – something that gave him great pleasure, like sarcasm. 'Oh! I didn't think it could be you that had left the cushions out in the rain.' Or 'The fridge dirty? Oh, I suppose the Queen is visiting – she's sure to look inside.'

He was particularly good at being supercilious and always so patronising of others. 'Dishonest,' he'd say. 'Well, we all get what we deserve. Frankly, I would never lie.'

Meryl found this self-righteous attitude difficult to live with because of course, according to Matt, no matter what, it was somebody else's (and usually Meryl's) fault. He never did anything wrong, though we all know that is unlikely to be true and a fly on the wall would attest to that. But according to him, Meryl was always responsible for their arguments. And right now, at this moment, his plan was to teach his pedantic wife a thing or two.

Meryl (and let's not think she was perfect, for of course it takes two to tango) was doing it silent over recent weeks – quite a dull and dozy time for a fly on the wall – as she was just unable to think straight after their last furious confrontation. She felt drained, an empty kettle, too exhausted for anger, quite devoid of energy for conversation even if she'd had anything to say.

Normally there was little repartee between them anyway, except for their disagreements, as they had nothing in common: he was addicted to football and she liked to write. He was indifferent to the pieces she showed him and she downright hated the winter months when the

TV blared from morn to night with large masculine bodies mauling and bashing each other over a stupid ball. She withdrew into herself, wandered through the daily routine and soaked up the sun in the garden. Colours absorbed her; the bright lime standing out against the deep viridian of the shadows on the grass made here aware that light can be found in every day, no matter how deep the darkness.

Lonely, she became creative, worked late into the night churning out poetry and short stories.

He would object to her absence from the living room with some sarcastic remark. 'Must be dating online the way you sit at that computer. Found someone handsome? A younger man, eh?'

These days she could let it roll. She even left off the vacuuming and sometimes it went for weeks before she tackled the mess.

Strangely, this was the last straw that led to Matt's decision. Now it dawned on him. He knew exactly how he'd fix this aggravating woman. Aggravating woman, a fly might ask. Ten years they'd shared their lives and all he'd got from it was a bitter wish to hurt and humiliate.

Next day, he rose early and for the first time in many months cleaned and polished the car. He rarely drove these days but he headed off in jaunty style, unlike his usually pessimistic 'it's sure to rain today' persona, returning some hours later still in fine form, smiling in a smugly satisfied way.

'So what have you been up to?' Meryl couldn't help asking as she finally began to vacuum the living room floor. 'And for heaven's sake wipe your feet. I've filled one bag already with all the muck on this carpet.'

'Nothing much,' came his non-committal rather jovial reply as he snuck into his den and closed the door.

She heard him on the phone but his voice was muffled, a hand held over the mouthpiece it seemed. Secret men's business.

Two weeks later, he was dead. Yes, it was sudden – a massive stroke, an ambulance ride and that was it. Meryl was certainly shaken. Everybody was, Matt having been in reasonably good health. But perhaps they could all see a little ray of sunshine rising ahead for Meryl. Time to relax, get rid of the old armchair, and enjoy the pleasures of domestic bliss! But no! Not quite yet…

A few weeks later, Meryl could be heard on the phone sounding hugely agitated and angry. Extraordinary, thought the fly, woken from his new regime of regular afternoon snoozing. What could possibly be wrong now?

The line reverberated with excruciating hatred.

'That bastard!' she hoarsely screamed, 'that bloody bastard, I could kill him if only he were alive. Do you know what he's done now?'

The mind boggled at the impossibility of Matt doing anything at this stage and who wouldn't be speechless?

'His will – his bloody will – he's instructed that his ashes are to be spread all over the living room carpet, and as if that isn't enough, the executors have to be witness to the whole performance. Can you believe anyone could be so, so, so…' She too was grasping for words. 'Just like it always was,' you could feel her shaking through frustrated tears, 'he had to have the final say on every single issue.'

Ah, but there he made his final mistake. In the end, it was Meryl who came out on top – after she eventually cooled down. Yes, she happily distributed the ashes over the carpet, thicker where his chair used to be, and then out came the vacuum. Oooh! How she pushed and shoved and rubbed with that machine, muscles strong and flexing. She went over and over every inch of the carpet, teeth gritted, grimly smiling. Even her grunting seemed to have a sound of pleasure as she put every ounce of energy into the job until each last, grey, skerrick was sucked up. Finally she maliciously (a fly might even say triumphantly) grabbed that bag, slammed out through the laundry door and hurled it into the garbage bin.

Oh, what a feeling! Oh Toyota, how she jumped, hands sky high, higher than any television ad. Layers of tension fell like slicing carrot with a peeler. A waterfall of joy sluiced over her cleaning away the years. Freedom beckoned and she suddenly felt like a million dollars.

Good riddance to bad rubbish, the fly would have heard her yelling. And he'd have seen her, hands on hips, legs apart, head thrown back, giggling her bloody head off.

Tomorrow was garbage day and off he'd go where he belonged with all the other muck in the bin. Well, thought the fly, this time she certainly did have the last laugh.

Sunday

How I love sleeping in on Sundays. Well, not actually sleeping – just floating in and out in a dozy kind of way. Especially in winter when I can pull the warm doona closer and wiggle my feet in the woolly bed socks Gran knitted me.

This Sunday, I was just snuggling up a bit more when Mum's yell penetrated my cosy cocoon.

'Rosie! Get going. It's your turn this week.' I groaned. Oh no! It's not fair. Why do we have to do this? Please don't make me, I pleaded, still in that dreamtime world.

'Come on. You've got five minutes or we'll be so late all the food will be sold.'

'I feel sick – my throat's killing me,' I coughed hard.

'Yes – pigs might fly,' she called. 'I'm in the car.'

I heard the front door rattling, opening loudly and Em in the bed beside mine snickering. Flinging clothes on, I angrily flipped her nose, grabbed my sneakers, slammed the door and flounced into the front seat.

'For goodness sake, Rosie, you only come about once every couple of months. Surely that's not too much to ask. I go every week.'

'Yeah, well you *want* to go and I don't and that's the difference. None of us want to go, except maybe Dad. Jenny doesn't, Em doesn't, Maxy hates it, you know that, and what about Ben – though you let him off half the time.' She knew none of us ever want to go, that we'd never tell our friends or anyone at school about these Sunday expeditions.

Mum was exasperated and I knew I was about to get a lecture on how lucky we were and how terrible it was for Donny with no family in Australia and surely if I was in his place I'd appreciate…and on and on she'd drone while I'd sit hunched up stonily filled with self-pity.

The only plus about the whole thing was the barbecue brunch – great steak and eggs – if we didn't miss out on the meat, which could happen at times. There was always a queue waiting to throw their stuff on the hot plate and then grabbing a bench to sit on. And of course, then there was Donny. I squirmed trying to avoid the unavoidable. Silent, broken, Donny.

I felt tearful suddenly. Why today? I don't know. Maybe because I could see Mum's determined face as she held hard to the wheel and I saw her goodness. I felt mean, though still disgruntled, but idly began to wonder how it would be to be Donny. Not all that much older than me with a wife and baby back home. Half a world away. I pictured the poor girl waiting. Waiting for her stupid man.

Her man who said, 'Don't worry, kiddo, it's foolproof,' as he kissed her goodbye. 'Be back before you know it. Then we'll be rich. Rich! We'll have a house and holidays.' Happy as a dog with two tails, he laughingly rubbed her cheek.

The enormity of it hit me. How to ruin a life in one easy lesson.

Just then the high barbed-wire fences came into view and the large concrete gates. I shivered at the chilling words in stark black lettering: Goldfield Gaol. Sunday is visiting day.

Technology PM

The rules were that each night all citizens must tune in to station Polylife.

On screen we watched the huge Mouth giving orders for the next day. Mouth was the deputy PM. She, the leader, is never seen. Will never be seen. We obey her ruling or rue the consequences. Screen Scene is what we call her.

Work schedules for the following day begin at 17.30 hours with the ten-year-olds, who must be asleep by star-shine. We are all micro chipped so our movements can be monitored and any child not closed by then in their ixcon, a steel cocoon, will be refused their red pills. These energy boosters also maintain the muscle tone needed for pulling heavy loads to build the Magaton, and any lagging youngster is zapped with biting electrical rays.

From then on, work is distributed for each age group. Now in my seventies, it is often hard to stay alert while the others are instructed quite late into the night. I struggle to maintain my physical strength, for as soon as I lose it, I will be disposed of. We do not know how this happens; the old people just disappear. We have never seen them going – they are just no longer with us. Some say they are mashed up for fertiliser needed for growing the herbs from which the pills for our survival are manufactured. I cannot dwell on it.

Those who are ill are used as human guinea pigs. They learn from these experiments how many pills are needed for optimum performance. There is great urgency in the Power Group to get the tower built from which to launch the space station, the Magaton, for its journey to Pomona. That is the destination for the Chosen Ones who will begin a new life on a planet where there is fertile land and abundant water. Earth is now completely devoid of water, which can only be obtained from a secret source. The Underground Resisters call on She, our faceless PM, to divulge the source of this water, but Screen Scene will only ever say that they, the Power Group, have a clear plan for the future, determined to support all those who are doing it tough. Ha. The Chosen Ones maybe.

The only future left for me is to find my beloved children. I am frantic to do this before I am disappeared. I don't care about me. I'm old and have had a lucky life, living in the time of plenty before technology imprisoned us and we killed our earth. I exist now only to share some precious moments with them. But how to do this, when human communication is disallowed – we see no real eyes, hear no real voices – is beyond me. I am beaten by science and its faceless robots.

I was only allowed two hours sleep last night after each age group had received their orders – building the tower and the Magaton is going at breakneck speed and we are all stretched beyond our limit. But in that short time I had a dream.

Such a perfect dream. It was miraculous and joyful so that this morning I am almost happy. I was with my children and grandchildren – we were celebrating something, I don't know what, but we were all together. We shared laughter, real food, clear water and…simple love. Maybe that dream is all I can cling to if I cannot find them. Or is it time to let go and allow 'them' to dispose of me?

The Lodger

Billy was pretty proud of his chooks. This last year he'd just about supplied the family – well, Mum 'n' Dad and him – with eggs. And not just ordinary ones. These were extra large, extra smooth, super tasty, best-in-the-world eggs. They all agreed.

'These eggs of yours, Bill,' Mum said, as she stoked the old fuel stove, 'are really something.'

'Good on yer, son,' said Dad, 'yer got yerself a nice little gang of layers there.'

Billy could feel his chest expand with pride. Praise from Dad was rare. He'd picked up his motley collection – first Maisie, a rather scraggy Red Australorp, and later Lola, Bess and Sue, of indeterminate breed – from various sources. Maisie just appeared one day. Kept pecking round the back door and when Mum threw out a few scraps, that was the end of it. They had her for keeps. Dad and Billy put together a makeshift pen. A coupla sheets of old corrugated iron, a few bent and rusty stakes, some holey chicken wire and Bob's yer uncle, Maisie was happy as a lark. And from then on laid a beautiful soft brown egg every day. Not long after, people up the road moved out and left their three hens to fend for themselves.

'Na, boy, them 'ol' things'll never lay. Fergetit.'

'Aw, go on, Dad, I'll get 'em ter lay,' pleaded Billy. And he did. Heaps of TLC, long heart-to-heart conversations, soft nests and good feed.

His girls all got on like a house on fire until the day when Rodger arrived. Rodger the Lodger, Dad called him. He flew in right over the high netting fence of their now new, upmarket, chook yard.

'Well, I'll be blowed,' Mum pondered. 'Ow the devil did 'e do that?'

He was a real cocky little fella, this Rodger, good-lookin' no denying, but he flustered the girls no end. Maisie's eggs got smaller and smaller and Lola gave up laying completely.

Dad was all for a quick execution and a special Sunday dinner, but Mum was aghast at that; she'd got quite fond of their new lodger and so…well, he backed down, and they agreed to put an ad in the local to try and find his owner.

Needless to say, nobody claimed him and meanwhile he puffed and strutted around generally ruling the roost. But strangely, in due course, the girls got used to having a man about the house and settled back into a contented and productive routine. Billy was even able to sell a few eggs to Mrs Donovan next door. So, as Dad said, old Rodger the Lodger had become more of an asset than a free-loader. Mum was pleased his early morning cock a doodle doo worked better than the alarm getting Dad out of bed to do the milking, and Billy was happy too – now he always had warm creamy milk on his porridge for breakfast.

The Weed

Blood oozed down her shin – soon it would melt into her sock. She didn't know what hurt the most – her bottom, which hit the edge of the step first, or her leg. Seeing the fresh flow of bushfire-red, she couldn't help crying out and was astonished at the sound. Did it come from her? That vampire howl? Sobbing and rubbing her bum, she struggled to her feet hoisting the heavy school pack over a bony shoulder. She hated the stupid great thing and no wonder – what little skinny nine-year-old body wouldn't?

Hardly knowing what to do and utterly exhausted after the fight, she stumbled out onto the street, part blinded by her tears. She rarely cried these days, determined not to let her grandmother get the better of her, but right this moment she felt mindless. She could be that broken yolk oozing across the lino bewildered now it was out of the shell with nowhere to go. Defying her grandmother, she scuffed her shoes along the pavement, feeling she was peering through a windscreen without wipers until she tripped, landing on top of her pack beside a brick wall.

The streets were empty, the sun hardly up, and she was glad Nancy, her new friend, couldn't see her in such a mess. She sniffed up hard and wiped her snotty nose across a grimy sleeve. The sock had soaked up most of the blood and the rest had become a dried black river. Dazed, she slumped, staring at nothing, all energy seeping out of her. A darting lizard made the day come into focus and her swollen eyes rested dully on a poor miserable weed growing in the crack of the wall. How on earth could it live there? About to pull it out, she hesitated.

'Hello, weed,' she trembled. 'You're just like me, aren't you? Nowhere to grow and nobody to look after you.'

Another bout of tears drizzled down her face and she leant over to let them drop on the barely green leaves. She thought she heard a thank you and saw a smile as she noticed a tiny bud snuggled in the straggly stem. It would be a miracle if it ever grew without good soil and water, but perhaps her tears would help. The thought took her back to a day spent with her mother planting carrot seeds and being told to be sure to add some of the compost from their special bin.

'I wonder what you are and what colour your flower will be,' she whispered gently. I wonder who I am and what I will ever be, she thought, but cloud seemed to cover the sun – it was too difficult to see past this moment. In the background, she still heard her raspy grandmother's angry shouting. Felt the strong fingers clawing into her arm, aware there'd be more bruises to hide.

And heard the yelling. 'Get out! Get out of here. Why in the hell have I got to put up with your shit? Just go. Get out and never come back.' And she had lunged and grabbed and pushed her out the door, chucking the school bag after her with an enraged heave.

'I'm sorry.' She'd tried to explain, searching for the dishcloth to wipe up the eggy mess. But it was no good. It was never any good. Gran had just ripped it from her hands and knocked her to the floor.

'And how many time have I told you not to use the dishcloth to wipe up the floor?'

Noises were beginning to arouse her from that place – the day was waking. Early birds were going about their early business and one of them was Merril, off to violin lesson.

'What you doing, Karl?'

Karley looked up, squinting against the light. Never cared much for Merril, who only seemed to be interested in the violin and was pretty uppity. But she got on the same school bus. She was ten and in the class above.

'Nuthin.'

'Can't be nothing. You're never here at this time. This is the early bus.'

'Yeah, well?' She turned away, hoping to hide her red eyes.

'Well nothing. What are you crying for? Do you want to come with me and get to school early?'

'Nup.'

Merril seemed to hesitate but saw the bus coming round the corner, shrugged and ran towards it. Karley felt bad. After all, Merril was only trying to be nice and nice wasn't something that came her way much these days. That set her to more tears. She wondered where they all came from. It was like a tap you couldn't turn off. If only she had a hankie, but they didn't come her way either. Her sleeve by now was totally disgusting and wiping it with a none too clean skirt didn't help – just made two yucky messes.

By now she could see the usual mob of workers and schoolkids beginning to trickle along the street. Impulsively scrambling over the wall, she watched the peak hour pouring by from inside the bushes. Ted and Gareth lumbered past, two of the bossy boys she tried to stay clear of, and then those stupid giggling girls in fourth class.

Finally here came her bus. Usually if she was late she would be in a panic but today there wouldn't be any school for her. She was quite calm about it – had no plans. Seemed to be looking at the world from another planet.

When her rumbling tummy reminded her she'd missed breakfast, she climbed back to share the warmth of the wall with her friend the weed. She sat close to it. Stroked the pale green stem. Marvelled that the tiny roots gave it strength to grow. She had tiny roots too or no roots – no parents, no little sister. She shuddered, allowing herself to relive that day when the terrible wall of fire blasted their lives to bits. The guilt was like being engulfed by a savage sea wave, a curling dumper. Choking and heaving to breathe, she saw it all again – replayed the movie, unable to turn it off. Why hadn't she stayed at home instead of going to Jenny's house across the valley? If she'd been there, they'd all be still alive – instead they are gone because they stayed, because they waited for her. It was all her fault.

'Sweetheart, I'd rather you didn't go today,' her mother had said. 'It's going to be so hot. Why not stay and play quietly with Bunsy?'

'I don't want to play with a three-year-old, I'm always having to play with her,' she grizzled. 'Pleeeease,' she entreated. And her mother had acquiesced.

'Oh Mum, I'm so sorry, she sobbed, and Dad and Bunsy, I'm sorry, so sorry – I want you back.' In her bewildered and battered grief, she found her hand clutching something. The weed! She had pulled it from its minuscule plot. Unbelievable horror raced like the fires through a body already smouldering with too many emotions. Today's friend. A friend struggling to get a life just like she was. Without a happy home. Only a lonely crack in the wall.

'Oh, no,' she wailed. 'I've killed you too.'

What made her rush across the highway nobody will ever know. The woman driving her daughter to school had no hope of missing that desperate lunge. She had wept beside the small twisted body. In agony held the limp little hands in hers. As kindly arms urged her away, she noticed a slim grassy weed coiled round the girl's fingers. Shattered like her windscreen she was further crushed by what she saw. A tiny bud, the beginning of life, but bent and broken, it was already wilting and resigned to die.

My Friend the Weed

whizzing past
i saw you
struggling between
vast concrete
slabs

hey you there
i send a
fleeting hello
then I am
past

into the rushing
day around
the roundabout
and down into
town

that was yesterday
today i
saw you again slowly
cruised to take
you in

sturdy seed unwanted
wiry weed
hell bent on survival
soaking up dew
drops

tomorrow what will
be will be
but i'll bet the bud will
burst into
flower

and you will
see the
master at work
making a
miracle

Uncle Harry's Ashes

After the funeral, they gave me his ashes. 'You were 'is favourite – put 'em where you like.'

Yes, they were right, I guess. I was the only one who had ever spent much time with him – but that was so long ago now, way back in my early teens.

'Silly old bugger,' they'd say. 'All 'e ever thinks about is 'is fishin'.'

I stayed with him often in school holidays, up at the shack, as he called it. Really wasn't a shack but neither was it the Ritz. I think I went to stay because Mum was at work, so it was easy for her to palm me off on him.

'Uncle Harry will have you,' she'd say, confidently, relieved I'm sure that I was off her hands. A bit tough of her, now that I think about it. Just took him for granted, offered nothing in return. Little thanks, no hand of friendship. She had no time for dropouts, especially not family ones.

It was OK by me of course. I didn't want to flop around in the flat bored out of my mind any more than she wanted me there. The shack was a far better option.

Uncle Harry had no rules and we just hung about. We both loved beachcombing and he had a great collection of flotsam decorating the yard: half an anchor, bottles, bits of timber (one with the letters INCESS crudely carved on it) driftwood, old coral and clam shells. I couldn't count the hours I contentedly spent sorting through his junk, romancing over dramatic shipwrecks and the fate of *The Princess* – how I pictured her brave bow ploughing into the huge waves.

Food was never an issue with Uncle Harry. As long as he had his beer and fish and chips every night, the world was sweet. 'Jesus, this is good stuff,' he'd wink at me as we sat on the sea wall crunching the batter and swigging it down with a XXXX. Meals from paper. No dishes. What kid wouldn't go for that?

'Now don't tell yer bloody mother I give yer this stuff. She wouldn't approve but it's what all young fellas need. Puts hair on yer chest.' He'd slyly grin and I reckoned he felt he'd got his own back on his uppity sister.

And who was I to complain? Soon learned to swill it down like a pro. Slurp, gulp, swallow, slapping the lips and wiping the drips with my wrist. Thought I was pretty cool.

And we fished of course. Every day. Come hell or high water.

Sad to say, poor old Uncle Harry was a lousy fisherman. Whatever bait he used or wherever we fished, we had no luck. Sometimes we dug up worms from the garden, stuffed them wriggling into an old IXL jam tin; sometimes we bought green prawns from the bait shop or used tiddlers he occasionally caught. Once, when we were wading in the shallows in the north corner of the bay opening oysters off the rocks and sliding them down our throats, a small octopus grabbed his ankle. What pleasure he had chopping up its tentacles.

'We gunna catch a biggie with this, boy,' he chuckled. But as usual only a couple of little throwback leatheries rose to the bait. His failure as a fisherman never worried him as far as I could tell and since he most definitely was not into cooking, it hardly mattered. He had his fun.

It was the dreamy, sunlit hours that enticed him; sitting on the breakwater, rod waiting, standing in the surf soaking up sea spray or out in the dilapidated old tinny. God, I would say to myself, if Mum could see me in this rusty barge, she'd have a purple fit. But the old outboard never missed a beat and I basked in the smells of salt and fish and sweat. I don't ever remember Uncle Harry having a shower. I certainly never did – the whole holidays. Guess the odd swim kept me from arriving home totally repellent.

They were good days for a kid with no father and I smiled as I sat on the rickety jetty hugging the box of ashes to my chest. Poor old codger. I hadn't seen him in years – too busy living, too selfish to give him anything but the briefest of thoughts – and now he was dead. And I was sorry.

Smiles of happy reflection changed as suddenly, inexplicably, tears began to roll down my cheeks. Unstoppable tears, tears for this forgotten, unremarkable, lonely, old man yet the one person in my life who had given me my youth, moulded my ways, started my journey.

'Gotta get educated, kid,' he persistently repeated. 'Never git anywhere without it. Don't wanna end up an old bum like me now, do ya?'

And I did what he said. Left those carefree days of life's lessons on the back road of my memory. Went to uni. Forgot all about Uncle Harry.

'God Jesus, Harry,' I choked. 'Jesus man, I'm sorry.'

'You OK, mate?' A firm hand touched my shoulder.

I looked up at a wrinkled, tanned face – noticed concern in his eyes and in those of the other fishermen staring across at me.

'Yeah. Yeah.' I shrugged, searching for the paper serviette I'd stuffed in my pocket.

And then the box was bruising my chest, reminding me why I was here. I'd planned to open the lid and throw the ashes across the ripples of the bay. Felt sure that it would please the old boy.

But how did I know? How did anyone know? Who had he last seen before he'd been found by a neighbour spreadeagled across the faded and chipping linoleum. Been dead for days, the ambulance men said.

Like a landslide, guilt clamped down on me, crushing, strangling my breath. He was older than old, since he seemed ancient when I was a kid, and we'd left him to battle on – indifferent, uncaring. We had abandoned him, allowed him to die, neglected and alone. Disbelief mingled with retching sobs. Shut your faces, you guys, I thought, leave me be, as I silently howled. But I loved you. I did. I really did.

I couldn't make myself open the box, hadn't a penknife anyway since my last international flight, couldn't bear to see the only remnants of his life. Unthinkable to touch them. I shivered at the thought and then began to uncontrollably shake, making the sunlight, spreading its gold across the water, crazily flicker and zag so that I accidentally dropped him in. The whole box and dice. Just jumped out of my hands – splash. While the blokes on the jetty pretended not to see.

Mesmerised, I watched as he floated away, peacefully like he would in his old tinny. Gently rocking with the tide's ebb and flow.

Clearly I saw him, gnarled, calloused hands hard on the tiller, deformed water-worn toes, curling under his feet, 'You 'ungry, boy?' he'd say. 'Git yer mug inter that san'wich then.' Four huge slabs with Vegemite. 'We don' hold on ceremony 'ere.'

Was OK with me. Glad to have a break from table manners.

I eased back against the post, calmer now, wrapped in the smell of briny memories, as he drifted to and fro under the jetty and back again, under and back, bobbing.

Cold shadows woke me: slowly, stiffly like the old man, I walked towards town, still blurry-eyed and runny-nosed, remorse weighing down each heavy step.

*

'What the hell have you been up to?' my cousin's voice shrieked across the line several days later.

'What do you mean?'

'What do you think I bloody mean? Harry's fucking ashes of course.'

'Harry's ashes?' I repeated dumbly.

'I've had the police battering down my door because of you. What the hell made you leave them on the beach?'

'I didn't…'

'They've been searching everywhere – asking crazy questions. What got into you? Made a real mess of things this time. Jesus, Steve, I don't know.'

I was still speechless. Couldn't get a word out. Dazed, my mind went blank, baulked at a repeat performance,

My cousin calmed down slightly, breathing into my silence. 'Oh well, forget it. I've made arrangements for their disposal.'

'Disposal?'

'Yeah. Apparently the trawlers go out nearly every day. One of them will chuck 'im over. About ten miles out. Should do the trick.'

Dispose? Chuck? Do the trick? God, is that all there it is to it? Icily beyond anger, I replaced the receiver, slowly bent my head to the table. Bereft, whispered, 'Goodbye, old fella, goodbye.'

Turn Back the Clock

Nothing could control her weeping. Not even Father's strong and loving arms, or Bonnie's wet nose nuzzling her leg. Even the staring silence of the other children. Her uncontrollable shaking became worse whenever she allowed herself a glimpse of Mother standing by the window. Through grimy tears, she saw her silhouette, motionless, stiff, cold and unforgiving, holding in her hapless arms the limp, wet body that just a sunny hour before had been laughing little John. She stood so still she might have been a statue bearing a lolling gollywog.

Millicent buried her head against this sight. To see him thus – her precious wee boy, her pet, her treasured baby brother – was inconceivable. She could never imagine life without him. She wanted to die too. To go with him to God in Heaven. For an instant she was suddenly still. God in Heaven? She moaned. God? Where was He this morning as they played by the river. How *could* He let this happen? 'I hate you, God, I hate you. Turn back the clock. I want it to be yesterday.'

'Shush, dear child,' Father choked through his own tears, gently stroking her clinging hair. 'We'll have to be strong, you and I. We must look after Mother. This is the second bairn she has lost. She will be needing all the care we can give her.'

'But what about me?' Millicent wailed. 'I loved him more than she did. I loved him more than anyone did.'

And there was no doubt she had. There'd been plenty of babies since she, the eldest, was born, but this one was different. Maybe because she was eleven, a bit older than when the others had arrived, magically it seemed, and like clockwork. Or perhaps it was because Mother appeared so tired and unable to cope with the demands of the other children that she had taken over the caring of this new baby, Johnny. Mother had given him the breast in the beginning but her milk had not flowed easily, so Millicent made sure she got the first let down every morning from old Elsie their faithful Jersey, and the little boy had thrived.

Yesterday they were playing in the sun near the vegetable garden. Presently they would pull the carrots, small and sweet, that he loved to chew on, but for now they were happy just feeling the winter warmth on their faces.

'Careful near the river now,' her mother had warned. 'You know how steep those banks are. And slippery,' she added for good measure.

Oh Mother, sighed Millicent – always worrying. Then the crow screeched – loud mean things, she hated their cruelty picking out the eyes of newborn lambs. Nearer it came, flapping those large wings so close that she grabbed her hat, waved and threatened, and for some seconds was blinded by the sun.

She went to take his hand. It was not there. The emptiness was suddenly terrible and ominous. She called, 'Johnny, Johnny, where…' running down the slope but in that instant her eyes focused on the circles in the river as if a large stone had been thrown. Small, neat circles at the centre, slowly widening getting larger and larger. A few floating bubbles glistened in their midst.

'No! No! No!' Her screams shattered the bland air. 'Help, help.' She fell, rolled, scrambled down over the dry grass and bruising rocks, then was caught in the tenacious branches of the willow weeping into the blue green water. Struggling to free herself, screaming still, and weeping, she hesitated to jump, heavily burdened by her long strong winter clothing. Clinging to a bending branch, she was unable to do more than take a few murky steps before the men arrived – Father, the two boys, and then the drover who'd stopped by for smoko. They stirred and muddied in their frenzied panic, making it impossible to see anything. Warily too, as none were swimmers.

But then Faulkner, himself only nine, called through brimming tears, 'I think…I felt something.'

And so it was. Father's long arms reached down and found a tiny foot, a foot that had lost its special new boot, and pulled the mud-covered toddler from the jealous river. Not so long without air in his lungs – but just too long. He was so utterly and absolutely not with them any more. Father gently pressed the small angel to his chest – his anguish too dreadful to watch.

In the shocked dead silence as they stood, dripping, half in and out of the water, numb and too devastated to move or speak, they looked up to see Mother standing on the top of the bank. Her glassy gaze beheld the scene but she spoke not a word. Made not a sound. Then slowly turned her back on the group below, and walked away.

The black crow flew above, shrieked his caw of death and disappeared from view.

Yellow Bird

'I do want a puppy.' She could wilfully manufacture in a second that wide-eyed look where a waterfall is about to flow deeply down the gorge. 'Please, Daddy, you promised, and I've had a name for ages. I'm going to call her Precious. Pleeeease.'

He lowered his large frame to the floor and hugged her close. 'Precious – that's my special name for you – Little Precious,' and he kissed her behind the ear.

She giggled and squirmed. 'That's why I chose the name. I'll feel better when you aren't here.'

How it hurt. His heart emptied out and floated from his grasp. He felt like a scooped out avocado – nothing left, just a hard dry crust. But what could he do? A job's a job. He stared inside himself – motionless until her voice brought him back.

'Daddy! Are you listening?'

He turned to her, an idea on his lips. 'You know you can't have a dog in this tiny flat but you could have a bird. I saw a gorgeous little yellow budgie in the pet shop just as I was coming home today. We could get a pretty wire cage and you could talk to it when you missed me. Why don't we go and see it in the morning?'

She stood dully, looking down on him as he sat hopefully on the floor.

The silence lingered until she shrugged and said OK in a passive, unenthusiastic way that left him no better off.

But the morning brought a sweetness that recharged his soul. She too fell in love with the little yellow bird. The pet shop lady gently placed the soft ball of feathers into her cupped hands, and they both smiled as the chirpy bright eyes darted from one face to another.

'I think she likes us.'The girl looked up.

'I think she does too,' replied the lady. 'She's finding it lonely without her little sister, who I sold a few days ago.'

They climbed up the stairs to the flat loaded with the bird in the cage and all the appendages to make a home for Precious. A feeder, a water container, a tiny swing that had to be had, and a mirror to act as the lost little sister. And seed.

'I can't wait to show Mama,' she said.

They found a spot for the cage on the bookshelf where morning sun would reach but left it cooler in the afternoon. The room seemed brighter, lighter, with this small piece of joy that was so full of life at any time of the day.

'Mama doesn't believe in God,' she said, 'but I think He sent Precious to keep us from feeling sad.'

He left next day, wrung out and lonesome but somewhat grateful for the existence of a little yellow bird. She had waved from the window, holding up the cage precariously but cheerfully, and he breathed in the flash of colour. Way out beyond, in the red earth and spinifex, countless miles from anywhere, he could smile at the memory and feel comforted.

It was a place for the girls now their man was absent and they became acclimatised to a routine. The happy little bird added cheer to the days; she was such a gift of love and made it seem that the man's presence was not as far away as it really was.

In the flat, mother and daughter argued about Precious.

'You spend more time talking to that bird than you do to me.'

'I'm sending messages to Daddy,' she chatted on, rubbing the small breast with her forefinger, something the bird seemed to enjoy.

'Mental telepathy, is it?'

'No, it's magic. Precious is magic, that's why we had to buy her.' She half-hummed, half-sang, her golden hair nearly matching the yellow bird as the sun filtered it's warmth into their world.

One morning a few weeks after the bird's arrival, the conversation turned to housekeeping.

'I think it's time you cleaned out the cage – it's quite disgusting.'

The girl could hear her father's voice, soft, deep, tender: 'You must care for her, Little Precious, make sure she has feed and water, and keep the cage clean.'

Obedient to both parents, she set to work. Just enough time before school, she thought.

'Come on, happy one, out you get for a little fly so I can clean up your room.' She gently set it on the back of the chair and watched, smiling, while the bird took in the freedom and joyfully flitted from chair to table top, to bookshelf, to vase, to fruit bowl.

Then her mother was calling, 'Hurry – we'll have to go or we'll miss the bus.'

But Precious was not to be caught, now she was feeling the fun of flight, the pleasure of space, the air in her feathers, and going back in the cage was not on her agenda. Usually when they let her out, she would calm down after a while and with some enticing bread they could get her back again. But now there was no time. Life had to be obeyed.

'I can't catch her. What'll I do?' she called.

'You'll have to leave her and come now – she can have a free day until we get back, though I expect she'll wreck the place.'

School and work took them away until they met again on the afternoon journey home. Opening the front door carefully, they squeezed in, fearful a streak of yellow would fly past, but all was quiet. There was no movement as they expected. No chirpy song. Just an awful foreboding quiet.

And then they saw it. Something like a scrap of yellow cloth dropped on the floor beneath the window.

The girl cried out, or tried to. 'No. No. No.' And rushed to cocoon the bundle in her hands.

In life, Precious was small but in death she seemed even more fragile and tiny. It was the absolute limpness that spoke the truth. The broken neck. Their broken hearts.

And there was yet another heart to break: a heart too far away. When the news reached him, the fog of leaving that had been lifted by the tiny, sunny spirit, descended again. Clung grimly. Gagged him with a vast loneliness.

'What's up with 'im?' mumbled a workmate.

'Dunno,' replied the other. 'Maybe 'is wife left 'im.'

How could they possibly grasp it when he, who now found himself grieving for two precious souls, was quite unable to do so?